Full-On Clinger

A LOVE ON TAP NOVELLA

LOVE ON TAP SERIES

SYLVIE STEWART

ROLLING HEARTS PRESS

ebook ISBN: 978-1-947853-17-1

Paperback ISBN: 978-1-947853-18-8

Also by Sylvie Stewart

To all my peeps back in North Carolina

Chapter One

"Are we gonna get wet?"

I flash my signature grin at the brunette with the smallest bikini in the group. And that's saying something.

"Only if I'm doing my job right."

Somebody's going to lose their bottoms before the afternoon is out, and I won't even need to lift a finger to make it happen—not that I don't plan on using all my fingers later tonight to drive Miss MicroBikini crazy. But I'll bet my left nut she's never met a class IV rapid, and neither has her scrap of a swimsuit.

Her wide eyes turn liquid as she lets her gaze fall down my body. *Yeah, that's it.* If I'm tightening my muscles a little, it's only because I just came from my morning workout and I'm still in flexing mode. Yeah, she likes what she sees, which makes all the time I spend working out well worth it.

I thought Brody and Josh were going to strain something trying to get an eyeful of my guests. A few choice curse words were flung in my direction as I made my way over to the waiting girls—God I love the week before graduation at SCUW. The bikini-clad co-eds come out in droves to enjoy the freedom of true adulthood and a fast-flowing Chattooga River.

Reluctant as I am to cut this little eye-fucking conversation short, I have a job to do. I clap my hands together and address the entire group. "Okay, ladies! Everyone put on your safety helmet and PFD, otherwise known as a personal flotation device. I'd hate to lose any one of you gorgeous girls to the river gods." This wins me a few giggles, just as I intended.

"My name's Denny and I'll be your river guide today." I pick up a paddle and flip it around with one hand as effortlessly as spinning a pencil. The move is well-practiced and always guaranteed to earn some smiles at the natural ease of my movements. "This here is your paddle. Not an oar. A paddle." I twist mine and bring the grip to a halt at my chest. "This is the T-grip. It needs to be covered with one hand at all times to keep you from knocking one of your raftmates unconscious and to maintain proper control while paddling. Control is crucial." I wink at a redhead in an electric blue bikini who's got her plump lower lip clenched between her teeth. I may have to invite her tonight as well.

I continue with my instructions—and my flirting—until I'm confident my delectable guests aren't going to drown or make me dive into the rapids at Bull Sluice after any of them. I hand out the paddles and more smiles. Damn, this is one fuck-hot group of girls.

But I've got two paddles left at the end when I should only have one. Somebody's missing. I do a headcount and, sure enough, seven beautiful ladies have turned to the riverbank where our raft awaits. I'm about to call out to Miss MicroBikini to ask where the last guest is when Brody jogs over with a hand up.

"Hey, man. Your eighth was hanging out inside. She's getting a vest on now." He stops with his hands perched on the waistband of his board shorts and lifts his chin. "I wanted her to learn the ropes from the best, so I went ahead and prepped her for you."

I bark out a laugh. "That's okay. I'll undo whatever you did in about thirty seconds."

Brody scowls. "No way, man. She'll see right through your pathetic moves and I'll be here when y'all get back. I've already laid the groundwork for a date tonight."

I haven't even seen this chick, but my competitive streak rears its head regardless. The brunette and the redhead have suddenly lost their new-girl shine.

"We shall see." I bump Brody's shoulder and he shoves me, but it's all good. This is how we operate.

"Denny?"

I turn to see the brunette has wandered back up the bank. She's definitely at least a 9.5 so I get my head back on straight and bring on the slow smile again. "Yeah, darlin'."

I swear I can see the moment the endearment hits because she does one of those little inhales that's like a tiny hidden gasp. She lowers her eyes for a second and then brings them back up to hit mine. "Can I sit in the back by you? You know, because it's my first time."

God-*damn*! I'd better watch myself or I'll be guiding this entire run with my dick standing straight up. I purse my lips like I'm thinking on it. Part of me is tempted to tell her she's more likely to get rocked around in the back, but the idea of her sitting close by when she screams is too appealing.

"Sure thing." I put her out of her misery.

"Chantal, if you want even the smallest chance of keeping your lunch down, you want to stay far, far away from the back of that damn raft." This comes from a new voice.

I turn to see who I assume is my missing guest walking toward Brody in a pair of short cut-offs and one of our standard red PFDs. I'm about to forfeit her to Brody on principle when my eyes finally reach her face and I lose the power of speech.

And it's not because she's abso-fuckin'-lutely gorgeous —which she is.

It's because my past just turned up to take a giant shit on what was looking to be a hell of a nice day.

"Rosie?" I finally choke out before clearing my throat. I take her in again, from the long legs to the curvy hips and on up past the shapeless vest to the nose that turns up just a bit at the end. Her tanned skin tells the story of a spring spent outdoors and the hair pulled back from her face reveals cheekbones I don't remember being quite so high. "What the hell are you doing here?"

She doesn't smile and neither do I.

"What the hell do you think I'm doing here?" She strides forward and grabs the extra paddle from my hand as she passes. "Going rafting, shithead!"

Shithead? *Shithead?* What the *hell?*

Rosina Carmichael has never once cussed in her life— at least not in front of me. And what's with that tone of voice? The Rosie I know—or *knew*, I guess—would never in a million years speak to me like that.

I turn and watch her walk away because it's the only thing I can do. My mind is so wrapped in confusion and surprise I hardly even hear Brody laughing his ass off at me. Rosie joins the assembled group, her dark ponytail swinging back and forth as she struts—yes, struts. There's no other word for it. One of the girls immediately grabs her arm and strikes up an animated conversation with her before they both glance my way.

The other girl wears a knowing grin, while Rosie's mouth is turned down. Her full pink lips are almost in a pout—the kind that makes a guy want to bite one of those lips.

I have clearly entered an alternate universe.

The last time I saw Rosina Carmichael, she did *not* look like this. Not even a little. And she most definitely did not talk like this, walk like this... *anything* like this. If I didn't know the impossibility of it, I would think this woman was a twin or maybe a really damn close relative. But those eyes tell me different. They're Rosie's eyes. The same ones that were brimming with tears the last time they met mine.

Brody grabs my shoulders from behind, his body still shaking with laughter. "Good luck with that." Then he shoves me toward the group of girls, sending me tripping over a tree root in the process.

Fan-fuckin'-tastic.

I'm torn between two instincts—the need to get as far away from Rosie as possible, and the opposing desire to get up close and personal with her to find out what the hell is going on. I have it on good authority that she'd never come seek me out until the day pigs decided to grow wings. Her appearance here is absolutely not a coincidence, however; of that, I'm damn certain.

Did Luca send her? It wouldn't really be like him to hide behind his sister, so I dismiss that one right away. And since my brothers and sister have given up, that leaves Mrs. Carmichael. That's much more likely—and probably scarier. If Adrina is getting involved, I'm up shit's creek—no pun intended.

But there's no time to catch Rosie alone so it's a moot point. As soon as the women begin choosing their seats, Rosie goes for the one the farthest as possible from mine—and one that will assure she'll get doused in no time flat. Typical.

Despite Rosie's warning, Chantal decides to stick with me and take one of the seats at the rear of the raft, right in front of mine. I just hope Rosie was teasing when it comes to motion sickness because we're in for a bumpy ride.

I brief the girls on where to place their feet to stay balanced and how to follow the strokes set by Rosie and the other girl in front. We practice shifting positions and paddling on land, as well as all the safety precautions before I tug the raft in the river and we all get started on our adventure. The tour usually lasts around five hours, a decent length for a bunch of first-timers—which has me questioning again why Rosie is on this outing with the bikini brigade. She's an experienced rafter, and I'd bet tonight's date with Chantal and the redhead that she does not own one bikini, nor has the word "amazeballs" ever passed her lips.

Chantal is full of chatter, very little of it about the breathtaking scenery or the river. It centers mostly on tales of Senior Week and questions about me. It seems half the girls in the raft are graduating and the rest are under-classmen in the same sorority or something. I'm trying to strike a balance between flirting with her and doing my job as a guide, but I'm not succeeding at either. So, I throw both out the window and cave to my burning curiosity.

"So, Chantal, how do you know Rosie?"

Her brow creases at first and then she frowns. "You mean Rosina?" She lets go of her T-grip and I motion for her to grasp it again. She pouts but does as instructed.

"Yeah. Rosina." It's been so long since I've spoken her name that it feels foreign on my tongue.

"She's friends with Gwen." Chantal motions to the girl sitting next to Rosie—the same one who shot me the knowing look earlier. What she thinks she knows is a mystery to me.

"She doesn't go to SCUW, though, does she?" It's admittedly been a while, but I have to believe I haven't put myself so far out of the loop that I don't even know where Rosie lives.

Chantal pouts again. "No. She goes somewhere else. Gwen invited her on the trip with us. Why? Do you know her?"

I give a noncommittal grunt. Do I know Rosie? That's a damn good question. I thought I did, but I clearly don't anymore.

At my silence, Chantal grasps the opportunity to change the subject. "So how long have you been doing this?"

I point out a rocky outgrowth and shout an instruction to keep up with the slow, steady paddling since we're on a quiet part of the river. I don't want them to use up the energy they'll need later. Giving into the subject change offers me a moment to think on Chantal's explanation.

I return my attention to her. "I've been here about two years. Before that, I was out in Colorado, but I grew up rafting around Asheville."

"Wow. So you really know what you're doing." She's out of rhythm with the other paddles, and I should call her attention back to the task at hand.

Instead, I wink at her. "I like to think so."

Her eyelids go heavy again and she lets her gaze drop down to my board shorts. I swear I could probably get her to do some naughty-as-shit things right here with everyone else on board. My eyes shoot to the rest of the guests as if I'm really considering getting something going, but whatever smile I'm wearing drops dead when my eyes meet Rosie's.

Her lips move as she mutters something under her breath and shakes her head. I straighten in my perch on the back of the raft, first feeling somewhat chastened and then feeling all kinds of pissed that she can make me feel that way. I'm not doing anything wrong. And I damn sure am not accountable to Rosina Carmichael—even though I've spent the better part of my life being made to feel I should be.

"What?" The word is out of my mouth before I can stop it.

I get the side-eye this time as she digs her paddle in the river. "Absolutely nothing."

God, she gets my back up. "You sure about that?"

"Yes, *Denver*. I'm sure. Now, how about we get this raft moving if it's not too much to ask?"

I bristle at her use of my given name. Her friend, Gwen, coughs out a laugh and Chantal pats me on the knee as if to reassure me.

"Hand back on the T-grip," I growl. I'm in no mood to flirt anymore.

If rapids are what Rosie wants, that's exactly what I'll give her.

My voice rises so everyone can hear. "The answer is yes, by the way."

I get a few quizzical looks but none from Rosie as she continues her paddling.

"Yes, what?" Chantal responds, just as I wanted her to.

My words are in answer to Chantal, but my eyes are

glued to the back of Rosie's helmet and the fall of dark hair extending below. "You're most definitely gonna get wet."

Chantal giggles and I swear Rosie's spine stiffens at my words. But she hides it by bracing her foot and pulling back on the paddle, starting a new rhythm to propel us toward the rough waters ahead.

Chapter Two

The first time Rosie Carmichael tried to kiss me I shoved her into the mud and made her cry. I got grounded for a week and I don't think I ever stopped resenting her for it. I was fourteen and had to sit in my room on the Friday night all my friends tried their first beer at Rich Flaherty's older brother's party out by Brickyard Road. Granted, if memory serves, they shared two cans of warm Old Style Light and wanted to spit it out, despite bragging up and down the next day about it.

But I blamed Rosie for making me miss a major milestone and for just being a general pain in my ass. She was all of eight years old, I believe, with dark bushy eyebrows, a lisp, and a determination to make me her boyfriend if it killed her—or me. My brothers thought it was a riot, but they weren't the ones being chased around by the little pest.

The fact that our mothers are best friends didn't help my cause one bit. Everybody thought it was cute as shit, this little girl following me around like a puppy, but it was fucking annoying and put a real dent in my street cred— something I was certain I had, even though I was just some kid from the decidedly non-street-cred-worthy mountain town of Asheville, North Carolina.

Suffice it to say, I was pretty much an idiot. But all boys are once they reach their teens. I like to think I've grown out of that, but my morning with Rosie and the girls from SCUW has proven one thing. Rosina Carmichael still has the power to drive me nuts.

We drag the raft up the bank at our designated rest stop and I pull out the cooler of waters and snacks that come included in the price of the tour. The women split into smaller groups, finding seats on shaded rocks or stripping off their gear and exposing a feast for my eyes. But I can't seem to enjoy it, even when the redhead and Chantal link arms and strut around in a show clearly meant for me.

Nope. All my eyes want is to latch onto a certain someone still hanging out with her helmet and PFD, her denim shorts soaked from the last rapid we traversed. The sun is shining and I can feel the heat here on the riverbank now that we don't have the breeze and the splashes of river water to cool us. I unclip my PFD and run a hand through my damp hair, all the while keeping Rosie in my sights.

There's something decidedly different about her, besides the obvious fact that she's grown into a woman and taken up waxing. Her eyebrows are perfect arches framing sky-blue eyes, and she's lost those Italian-bred sideburns I used to make fun of. *Yeah, I was a total prick.* My eyes drop down to her long smooth legs, their olive tone already dark even though it's only May. I wonder if her waxing routine includes... shit, I can not let my mind go there. I've known this girl since she was born, for Christ's sake. She's not only off limits, but she's absolutely not my type.

I'm surprised when she steps toward me, her eyes meeting mine. I figured she'd continue keeping her distance, but she's obviously got something on her mind. And if her frown is anything to go by, it can't be good.

"You just had to call me Denver, didn't you?" It's the first thing that comes out of my mouth.

She pauses for a second and I think I spot a tiny grin curving her pink lips. "Well, it *is* your name, you know." Her steps resume until only a few feet separate us. Rosie looks to her feet, probably trying to hide her smile.

I feel the unbidden urge to bend down so I can get the full effect of it, but I resist the temptation.

"I'm well aware, but just because *you* go by your full name now doesn't mean *I* have to."

She still doesn't look at me or respond. I shake my head and raise my eyes to the sky where the clear blue is bracketed on either side by towering evergreens.

"What are you doing here?" My voice is more exasperated than I intended, but I can't seem to help it. "And don't say you're here to raft. You could do this run in your sleep and I know you didn't travel over a hundred miles just to see the Chattooga."

A glance down shows her grinding the toe of her soggy tennis shoe into the dirt. She finally looks up and her smile is gone, replaced not by the perturbed look from earlier, but by something resembling sorrow. I want to back my ass up and dive into the river right this very second. That look can't bring anything but a bucketful of trouble.

Her brows draw together and her voice is hoarse when she speaks. "Denny, you need to come home."

I knew it!

I force out a laugh and pull my vest all the way off. "If that's why you came, you wasted a trip, darlin'."

She scowls at my throwaway endearment and I want to snatch it back, despite my raised hackles at her proclamation. I drop the vest on the cooler and cross my arms over my bare chest.

Rosie keeps her eyes on my face and I watch as her nostrils flare. "Don't think I don't know that. I told Mamma and Luca as much."

So Luca *was* in on this. I'd already figured Adrina was behind it, but Luca?

My hands land on my hips. "So why didn't Luca come himself instead of sending you?" I'm feeling a little pissed that my best friend couldn't man up and, instead, sent his little sister.

Rosie's eyes drop to my chest now, but her reaction isn't the one I'm used to getting from women. She narrows her eyes and lets out the kind of sigh that tells me she thinks I'm the biggest idiot on earth. "He has a little thing called a job. He can't just take off whenever he wants, unlike some people."

Now I'm good and pissed. "What the hell do you think I'm doing?" I gesture around to the raft and the flowing river behind me. "This happens to be a job if you haven't noticed."

But she has the nerve to completely ignore me. "Are you finished?"

No, thanks very much. I'm not.

I step closer and try keeping my voice low. "What about you? I see you've got time to flit about with the bikini brigade and have yourself a nice little vacation."

I can see her fists tighten at her sides as she speaks through clenched teeth. "I am not on vacation. I just finished my finals and I agreed to take my few precious days off to come and fetch your ass since you can't be bothered to return any phone calls." She leans in and I can see the ring of dark denim blue around her irises. "God, you're such a child!"

"Me?" I can't help my laugh. "I'm not the one throwing a temper tantrum on a river bank and butting into other people's business."

I swear she growls and for some reason I feel it in my dick. "It is my business when it affects the people I love." She shakes her head and looks ready to spit. "You only care about yourself. I knew this was a waste of time, so I'm just gonna lay it out for you and then we don't have to speak anymore. We'll finish this run and I'll get out of your hair so you can go back to being a selfish asshole."

There she goes cussing and yelling again. What in the hell happened to meek little Rosie? I open my mouth to hurl a retort or maybe a brilliant insult, but she cuts me off.

"Ginny is having her knee surgery on Thursday. Everyone is going to be there. Everyone but you. She won't tell you, but it's breaking her heart that you're not even acknowledging it—or her, for that matter. It's the least you can do to get over yourself for one minute and go home to see your mama."

She's right up in my face but I try not to let the words hit me. I can't think about my mama right now. I can't let my mind go to my family. I've spent the last four years training my brain not to go down that rabbit hole. But here Rosie is hauling everything out from behind that carefully closed door in my head and heart. I knew from the moment my eyes hit her this morning that she was going to turn my day upside-down—I didn't anticipate her trying to turn my carefully constructed world over while she was at it. There is no way I'm letting her do this and there is no way I'm talking to her about my family.

Her eyes are blazing with fire and challenge. I erase the space between us, expecting her to back down, but she doesn't. I'm about to tell her to go find her way back to the boathouse on her own when I catch her almost impercep-tible glance down at my mouth. My words catch in my throat and I can feel her quickened breaths on my chin. I'd have sworn her intensity was due entirely to anger and frus-tration, but that tiny glance tells a different story. One my libido has taken particular notice of. When her lips part the smallest bit, I throw all common sense out the window and bend down to do the last thing on earth I ever thought I'd do—kiss Rosina Carmichael.

Her lips relax under mine as I cover them. She smells like sunshine and the river, but she tastes like the first bite of a ripe peach. Her full lower lip is between mine and I slant my head for another taste. The kiss is more than a little awkward with her helmet on, but I don't give a shit.

I'm not thinking about anything but the taste of her and the feel of those silky soft lips against mine. I reach a hand up to touch her, but before I can even brush one finger across her skin, both her hands hit my chest and she pushes me away.

"What are you doing?" She wipes the back of her hand over her lips as if she's tasted something foul.

Okay. Not the reaction I normally get.

It's only then that I remember we're surrounded by seven hot women, all of whom have just witnessed the whole kiss/shove/sewage-sandwich-hand-wipe scene. Terrific.

I've been known to flirt and take a guest out before, but it's never kept me from doing my job. I feel like I've crossed several lines at once, not the least of which is kissing the very girl I swore I'd never in my life lay a hand—or mouth—on. What is wrong with me?

So I choose to go to one of my main areas of expertise and shove the entire thing to the back of my mind, doing my best to pretend it didn't even happen. I paste on my most charming smile and bring my hands together in a loud clap.

"Okay, ladies, break time is over! Let's go hit those rapids, shall we?"

Chapter Three

Chantal gives me the silent treatment for the rest of the tour. It's probably for the best anyway, since I'm in no mood to work my moves on her or anyone else for that matter.

Apart from Rosie's friend, Gwen, I seem to be persona non grata with this crowd. She's sent me a few commiserating looks I'm unsure how to take. Rosie hasn't even looked at me since we got back in the raft, and the rest of the girls are chatting between the shouts and squeals when we hit some good rapids. We still have Bull Sluice to go, and I'm not sure the group is ready for a class IV. I generally ask my guests if they want to opt out and I'll be doing the same today.

"Bump!" I shout when I see an upcoming rock. To my surprise, the entire group reacts exactly as I demonstrated in the intro lesson earlier. We easily pass by without anyone falling out of the raft. "Great job, ladies!" Maybe they can handle it after all.

Not a single smile or response comes my way. It's a shame, really—all this hotness wasted by the appearance of one cranky blast from my past. Brody and Josh will eat this up for sure. The tour can't end soon enough, as far as I'm concerned, so I dig my paddle in to bring us closer to Bull Sluice and the end of this torturous run.

Twenty minutes later it's decision time so I bring us to the river bank for a talk. Chantal and the redhead, whose name I've learned is Courtney, are still not looking at me, and Rosie has her arms crossed over her vest, but the rest of the women appear to have forgiven me for whatever transgression I've made.

I clap my hands together again to get everyone's attention. "You all have a choice now, and nobody's going to think any less of you if you opt out, but Bull Sluice is up ahead and it's a class IV rapid." This gets even Chantal and Courtney's attention. "It's considerably tougher than anything we've crossed yet and it has a nice drop where everyone is gonna get soaked. You'll have to be sharp, listen to instructions, and paddle your ass off, but I promise it will be worth it." I can feel myself smile and I'm almost back in my groove. "It's a hell of a ride." There's nothing like the adrenaline kick from negotiating a tough rapid. Well, almost, anyway.

Gwen raises a hand first. "I'm in."

She's followed by a few more "Me too"s and a couple "Hell yeah"s. Rosie offers no comment, but before I know it, all eight are grabbing their paddles, everyone with a hand on the T-grip and a determined stride. If I were the type to do such a stupid thing, I might shed a tear or two.

"All right, then. Let's go ride some rapids!"

As Rosie passes by me, I'm tempted to put an arm out to stop her. I'm trying my best to pretend this day hasn't been weird as shit, but it's damn hard when she's pouting her lips and moving those long legs every which way. Not to mention the taste of her still lingering on my tongue long after my lips caught hers.

But I don't. Because any interaction with Rosie will only lead to me dragging up a history I'd rather keep buried. Much better to enjoy the breeze, the sound of the birds singing, and the flow of the river. And if I'm lucky, I'll get to end the day with a beer and my feet up on the railing of my tiny front porch.

High fives and whoops echo off the steep rock walls as my team of women celebrates passing through Bull Sluice like a bunch of pros. I feel like I owe them all a damn apology for doubting them for even a second. They've removed their helmets and Chantal and Courtney are doing some kind of dance that should make my cock stand at attention, but all I can feel is pride. Even Rosie is smiling as she watches the show. Before I can think about it, I sidle up beside her and give her an elbow to the PFD.

"Not bad. Not bad at all."

She tilts her head to me and her grin turns a bit smug. "Not such a bunch of delicate flowers after all, huh?" Locks of dark hair have escaped her ponytail and lie plastered to her cheeks. I pull back on my urge to tuck one behind her ear.

Instead, I shift my mouth to the side and unbuckle my vest. "Well, you have to admit, the day did start off a little rocky." I'm not even sure if I'm talking about the flirtatious women or Rosie crashing my tour.

She considers me for a minute as she unbuckles her own PFD and slides it off her shoulders.

My mouth goes dry as ten-day-old toast as I get my first look at what's been hiding under her vest this whole damn time. A wet aqua blue Biscuit Head t-shirt clings to her every curve, accentuating the swell of full breasts, a narrow waist, and the exquisite flare of hips that beg for a man's hands. She tosses the vest on the nearby pile and I catch the phrase printed on the back of her shirt.

Put some south in your mouth.

Good God.

My eyes drop from the shirt to her ass in the wet cut-offs and I bring a hand to my mouth to confirm it's not hanging open.

Since when does Rosina Carmichael have curves like that? Last time I saw her she was wearing a shirt three times too big for her and had a build that reminded me of my younger brother, Miller—scrawny, narrow, and flat as a board. How could four short years produce such an astounding transformation?

Rosie turns and I swear she catches me gawking but I can't give one good goddamn. She's hot as all fuckin' hell —something she must know.

But she's not playing and there's no smug smile

anymore when she swipes back the errant locks of hair and tightens her ponytail.

"I'm catching a ride back to Asheville tomorrow with Gwen." Her hands perch on her hips and she looks me dead in the eye. "I can't pretend to know how you feel, Denny, but I'm begging you—for your mama's sake—please come home. Even if it's just for a few hours."

I don't respond. I can't. I'm still taking in this new Rosie and trying to shove shit back.

Chantal lets out a shout as she swings Courtney around, drawing both our attention.

"Pushing people away doesn't make them love you any less. And I'll bet good money it hasn't changed the way you feel about them either."

It doesn't escape my attention that she used the word them instead of us. And why wouldn't she? I never gave her any reason to think she meant anything to me. She was nothing but a thorn in my side—a full-on clinger when all I wanted was to hang out with my friends and make out with hot girls.

"Hell, of all of you, I reckon you love your mama more than anyone."

I dart my eyes to her. "Now, what the hell would make you say that?"

She goes for the sigh again—the same one from earlier that tells me I'm only a small step up from an orangutan on her own personal IQ scale. It's like she can't help herself.

"I'm not stupid, Denny." She smooths her hair back again and watches as two of the other girls join in the dancing. "And neither is anyone else back home."

The squeaking brakes of the outfitter bus tell me our ride is here, but I'm not done with this little conversation. Rosie takes a step toward the ridge and the waiting bus, but I move in front of her and grab her arm. Her skin is warm and soft, but I try to ignore how it feels against my palm and fingers.

"You seem to think you know a lot about me, Rosie. But my life is perfect just as it is." And it's true. I get to do what I want when I want, and I don't form attachments to people or things anymore. I live simple and take life one day at a time. "I'm not looking back."

She meets my eyes again and I swear she's trying to get a peek inside my brain she's straining so damn hard. But there's nothing to see. I've already spoken the truth. When I left home four years ago, I didn't look back. And even if I wanted to—which I don't—they'd never forgive me, so it's not worth sparing it even a single thought.

Yet Rosie continues to stare until I can't take it anymore and I break both our eye contact and my grip on her arm. I watch the group of women as they gather all the paddles and vests without me even having to ask. I turn to help and Rosie's voice hits me square in the back.

"Maybe you need to adjust your expectations, Denny Brooks."

"Thanks, Denny. We had a great time!" Courtney shouts from the drivers' seat of a bright yellow VW Bug while three other girls wave from its windows.

I've had time to regain my composure, so I wave and send my best grin in their direction. "See y'all next time!" Despite my initial plans of procuring some evening entertainment, I'm content to watch them drive away. Two more of the women linger, talking to a grinning Brody and a wide-eyed Josh. That boy had better put his eyes back in his head or he'll never have a shot.

I carry a stack of paddles back to the boathouse and notice Rosie and Gwen standing beside a silver Jeep Wrangler. They appear to be arguing about something, but I pretend I don't even see them. Rosie's trip here was a fool's errand and I wish I hadn't even laid eyes on her.

The equipment has never been arranged so neatly by the time I finally come back outside. I tell myself my attention to detail has nothing to do with wanting to avoid Rosie, but I can't say I'm upset when I see the Wrangler no longer in the gravel lot and Brody and Josh the only people still milling around. My chest feels a little tight, but I chalk that up to not eating enough today.

"Yo!" Brody lopes over, his shaggy blond hair a tangled mess and his tall frame eating up the distance in no time. He's got his phone in one hand and holds it up to me. "That Gwen girl wanted me to give you a number."

I feel my brows draw together. Gwen? Now, *that*, I didn't expect. I shake my head but he waves me off. "Not Gwen's number. Rosina's. And thanks, by the way."

The sarcasm isn't lost on me. "For what?" I cross my arms over my chest and wait for whatever bullshit is coming.

"For ruining my date with Rosina. You obviously

pissed her off with whatever the hell you did today. I couldn't even get a word out of her when they came back."

My spine straightens like a nun's ruler and I take a step toward Brody before it even registers what I'm doing. "Not in this fucking lifetime or any other." I'm practically growling and don't recognize my own voice.

Instead of being intimidated, Brody throws his head back and guffaws. "That's what I thought."

I turn and stalk back to the boathouse, my head a tangle of conflicting urges and thoughts.

"I'm texting you her number!" Brody calls out after me. "Gwen said they're staying on campus tonight but they'll be leaving in the morning!"

Morning can't come soon enough, as far as I'm concerned. Then I'll be rid of Rosie and her damn presumptions for good.

Chapter Four

The phone rings on the other end for the fourth time and I can feel the sweat forming on my palm where I grip the plastic case.

Fuck. This was a stupid idea.

I let the phone fall to my lap and am about to hit the end button when I hear a familiar voice on the other end.

"Denny?" Her tone is sleepy—and why shouldn't it be? It's going on three a.m. and any sane person is fast asleep right now. Except for me. And, now, my baby sister.

"Hello?" Her voice comes a little louder this time, followed by a mumbled, "Please don't let this be a damn butt dial," that brings an immediate smile to my face.

I lift the phone back to my ear. "Hey, Lynnie."

"Oh my God!" she practically squeals, and I feel my chest loosen the tiniest bit.

It seems it wasn't my lack of breakfast that was causing my chest to feel tight all evening. The big-ass burger and sweet-potato fries I downed for dinner proved this by doing nothing to ease it, and by the time I went to bed I was half convinced I was gonna have a heart attack.

I got up the first time at one and tried doing some pushups and chugging a glass of water. At two, I turned on the TV and had a beer. And for the last half hour, I've been sitting on the edge of my bed holding my phone and cursing up and down until I finally admitted defeat and dialed Lynn's number. I reckon she's the least likely to murder me in my sleep and the most likely to keep her damn mouth shut.

"Keep your voice down, will ya? I don't want you waking the whole house."

Her voice drops to a whisper. "Sorry. I'm just so happy to hear your voice."

Well, shit. I mean, it's not like I expected her to spit into the phone, but I never thought she'd be so... cheerful.

"Good to hear yours too. What have you been up to?"

The question is ridiculously inadequate, but she doesn't miss a beat.

"Mama grounded me 'cuz she caught me making out with Ben Weller in the backseat of his car." She lets out a half-laugh/half-groan and I switch the phone to my other ear.

"Ben Weller? Little Ben Weller from Haw Creek?"

Lynn snickers. "Not so little anymore, if you know what I mean?"

I almost drop my phone, but the sheer force of my shock keeps it in my hand. "Jesus, Lynn! What the hell?"

She's outright laughing now. "Don't get your panties in a twist. I'm just kiddin'. Well, kind of."

I growl for the second time today and stand from the bed. "Kind of, my ass! You tell that kid he'd best keep his hands to himself if he wants to live to see... wait, how old is he anyway?"

"Duh. Seventeen, Denny. Same as me."

This hits me like a bullet to the gut. It's not like I don't know how old Lynn is; it's just that I haven't allowed myself to think about it long enough to picture her as anything but the lanky thirteen-year-old she was when I left.

Hell, Luca's the only person from home I've stayed in touch with, and that's just because he's not blood and he's the most stubborn person—besides me—that I know. There was also that one time Cash came to hunt me down when I got back from Colorado, but that's not worth rehashing.

"Well, he won't see eighteen if he takes you out in his car again. What were you thinking anyway? Mama must be fit to be tied." I'm pacing the wood floor now.

Lynn tsks in my ear. "I was thinkin' the exact same thing you were when Gretchen Seager's mom caught you and her nasty-ass daughter in the bed of Daddy's F150!"

How the hell did she know about that? And Gretchen wasn't nasty. She was just... well, all right, maybe she was a tad waspish. And then there were those awful fake nails. But the girl sure knew how to use her... "You don't know what you're talking about. For God's sake. What do Miller and Cash have to say about this?" I can't imagine my brothers would let this slide.

"Please. They don't know a thing. I'm a sweet little

lady, don't you know?" I can practically picture her polishing her imaginary halo over the line.

Jesus. Isn't anybody keeping Lynn in line?

A voice from the back of my head scoffs at that. *You should be the one taking care of her, asshole!* I push it aside.

"Well, at least you have Mama to keep an eye on you."

Lynn goes quiet and I know I've finally touched a nerve. I'm amazed it's taken so long.

"Hey." I stop pacing and keep my voice soft and steady. "She'll be all right. It's just knee surgery."

I finally get a quiet response. "I know."

We're both silent for several long seconds.

"Don't you let your head go there. It was a fluke—nothing more. Just one of those things."

The unmistakable sound of sniffling crosses over the airwaves. *Dammit.* That tightness is back and it's more constricting than ever, threatening to steal both my voice and my breath. But I can't leave her hanging. I just can't—which is preposterous given that it's exactly what I've been doing to all of them for the past four years. Since the day after my dad's funeral. The same day Rosie begged me to stay and I left anyway.

I force a confident tone. "You know Mama. She'd march up to St. Peter and demand he call her a taxi if she ever reached those pearly gates. And he'd do it if Mama said so—you know it as well as I do."

Her laugh is watery. "You did come by your stubborn streak naturally, I suppose. You and Mama are two peas in a pod."

"Damn straight!" I patently ignore the second part of her comment.

There's another moment of silence and I hear her blow her nose before coming back to the phone.

"Denny?"

"Yeah?"

"Are you calling because you're coming home, or are you calling because you're not?"

Shit. The last thing I want to do is hurt my baby sister, but I don't have it in me to go there. So I take the easy way out.

"You don't need me there. Remember, Mama's gonna be just fine." When Lynn doesn't respond, I add, "And anyway, I'm scheduled to work." Which is the absolute truth, but it's also the thing that makes me an absolute prick.

Her voice is quieter still when she finally responds. "Sure. I understand." I don't like the artificial tone she'd adopted. "I gotta go back to bed. You know, school tomorrow."

"Oh, right." I hadn't even thought of that, but I know it's not the reason she's ending the call. "Hey, you take care and make sure you tell Ben Weller to keep his hands to himself."

"Love you, Denny," Lynn says. She hangs up before I even have a chance to decide what I might say in return.

I get a couple restless hours of sleep before I give up entirely and throw on a t-shirt and a pair of shorts for an early morning run. The sounds of the forest usually do such a thorough job at keeping me company that I don't need headphones and my phone to pump in music for distraction. I don't see the need to be distracted from all the sights and sounds surrounding me when it's just me, my footfalls, and Mother Nature.

This morning is different, however.

I can't get Lynn's voice out of my head no matter how loud the birds call back and forth, attracting mates and echoing against the canyon. Hell, even that notion makes me angry all over again about that damn Weller kid and his apparent death wish. I know it's a double standard, but I don't give a shit. I pump my legs harder in a futile attempt to outrun my thoughts.

Logically, I know I was right in what I told Lynn. Mama will be just fine. The chances of both our parents dying from complications with general anesthesia are probably about a million to one. And our mother is healthy as a horse—or at least she was when I left. She hikes and rides her bike and tends her giant garden, in addition to working full time. From the minimal info Luca forced on me, this knee surgery is probably due more to her acting half her age instead of any deterioration to be concerned with.

Still, I understand Lynn. Only all too well.

I wipe sweat from my face with the t-shirt I shed and tucked into the back of my shorts. It's still early but the air is warm and the sky is cloudless.

Half of me regrets calling Lynn and the other half is

treasuring the youthful lilt of her voice still resonant in my mind. The familiarity is clawing its way through my entire body like water through a fissure in a dam, and I'm afraid the entire thing will collapse if I don't fortify it right away.

I blaze faster down the dirt path, my breathing ragged as my body lets muscle memory propel me forward while avoiding the occasional tree root or rock. I don't even realize where I'm headed until I break through a clearing and see the boathouse.

I skid to a quick stop, kicking up a cloud of dust around me before I bend over and grab my knees. I'm breathing too hard—much harder than I should be from a morning run. Shit. Maybe I *am* having a heart attack. I drop to my ass and gasp for air. Of all the ways I thought I might go, lying in the dirt covered in pine needles and sweat isn't anywhere near the top of the list. I always figured I'd bite it over a waterfall or something equally spectacular—or spectacularly stupid, depending on how you look at it.

Blackness creeps into the edges of my vision and my head spins. Yup. This is it. I'm dying.

The last thing I hear before the blackness takes over is the sound of Lynn's voice telling me she loves me.

My immediate thought is one of surprise that the afterlife is so dark. I mean, you always hear about going to the light and all that crap, so I guess I wasn't prepared for darkness. I also wasn't prepared for the pain. Nobody warns you that your initiation into heaven involves an ass-kicking. Or... wait... shit! I should have anticipated this. Hell is exactly the kind of place you'd get your ass beaten at the door.

"Stop fucking around and get up!" This must be the voice of my official tour guide of hell. Funny, though, it sounds a lot like Brody.

It dawns on me that I have the ability to open my eyes and when I do, sure enough, there stands Brody, but he's silhouetted by a bright light behind him. The fires of hell, perhaps?

"I didn't know you had another job," I say, contemplating for a moment just how much a job in the underworld might pay before reality finally sets in.

I lift my hands to look at them and they're covered in dirt. "What the hell happened?"

I see his shoulders shrug and then he bends down to pull me up to sitting. "You tell me. I figured you were faking it. I guess I shouldn't have kicked you so hard." He lets go of me once I'm steady and scratches the blond scruff on his cheek. "Sorry about that."

I turn my head from side to side, testing for dizziness, but it's gone. My breathing has also returned to normal. Huh. That was really fucking weird.

"You need a doctor?" Brody's voice is laced with concern now that he's stopped beating me up.

I drop my face to my hands and groan as I remember it all.

"Shit. I'll call 9-1-1." I can hear the panic in his voice so I quickly wave him off.

"No. Don't. I don't need a doctor."

"You sure? What can I get you?"

I tip my head back and close my eyes, letting the rising sun spill down on me.

I pull in a slow breath and do my best to brace myself. "We can start with your phone."

Chapter Five

The second time Rosie Carmichael tried to kiss me I called her stupid. Well, technically, my words were, "Don't be stupid," but I imagine the effect was the same. She was having a sleepover party for her thirteenth birthday and my mother sent me over with a present. I was getting packed up to leave for college and wasn't about to say no to Mama. But Rosie somehow got me alone and tried to plant one on me. Thankfully, I saw it coming and ducked out of the way.

"What do you think you're doing?" She was a kid, for God's sake. And I was a man.

Her cheeks flamed red as she stood there in an oversized Kings of Leon t-shirt, her tangled brown hair covering half her face. "I figured since we're both teenagers now..." she trailed off, looking down at her bare feet.

"Don't be stupid, Rosie. I'm nineteen. You're just a kid." Yeah, I was the master of tact.

There was no mistaking the tears in her eyes when she

brought them up to meet mine. I felt like a total asshole. So I dropped my voice and put a hand on her shoulder, relatively certain I wouldn't be arrested for it.

"Hey. I'm sorry. I shouldn't have said that." I sighed, trying to think of what I could say that would get her silly crush to fade. I ended up going with the tried and true, "You'll find somebody who's right for you, you'll see. Then you won't even remember why you ever wanted to kiss some old guy like me."

Yeah, I was pretty sure I knew everything there was to know in the world at that point. I know better now how life can deliver a curveball faster than Sandy Koufax at his prime.

I lean against Brody's car with his phone to my ear while I watch him drag a kayak from the boathouse. He likes to fish whenever he can, and working for the outfitter provides the perks of free equipment and a couple trucks to haul it. For the second time in a few short hours, a sleepy female voice greets me over the line.

"Hello?"

This one hits my gut in an entirely different way than the last one, however.

"Mornin', Sunshine!"

I don't know why I call her that or why I'm acting so damn exuberant, but after my little bout of anxiety, I'm just happy my voice works at all.

I can hear the rustle of bedsheets. "Who is this?"

Ouch.

"Uh, LeBron frickin' James. Who do you think?"

"Luca?" The sleepy tone is replaced with a smart-ass one.

"Close, except I'm better looking and not a douchebag."

"Hmm." Another rustle of sheets. "Brody?"

I narrow my eyes and flip the bird at Brody's back, even though he hasn't technically done anything.

"You know, you could be a bit nicer to me, considering the reason for my call."

That shuts her up.

I take a gulp from the water bottle Brody forced on me and wipe my mouth.

"Cat got your tongue?" I'm surprised at how calm I feel.

"N—no. I'm just a little shocked, to be honest."

I deserve that, no doubt about it.

A door closes on her end. "Does this mean what I think it means? Are you coming home?" The hope in her voice threatens to undo me.

I take another breath and run my finger along the plastic label on the bottle before setting it on the hood of the car. "I'm thinkin' on it."

Her voice is almost breathy when she responds. "Really?"

"Yeah." My eyes follow Brody's steps as he comes back to the boathouse for more equipment.

"It will mean the world to Ginny. To everyone."

Dammit. I wish she hadn't said that. I feel the pressure of expectations caving in on me and I groan.

"Denny?" There's that hopefulness again, but it's tinged with disappointment this time.

"It's just... a lot." I grip the back of my neck and close my eyes. "I need a couple days. You go on home."

"No!" she practically shouts and then hurries on, "Come with us. We're leaving today and it will give you time to visit with everyone for a couple days before the surgery."

"Eh. I've got stuff to do around here." I don't tell her that I have today and tomorrow off, but I *am* scheduled to work Thursday through Monday, so it's not really a lie.

She sighs and, despite my inner turmoil, I can't help but imagine the shape of her lips. "You still seem to be laboring under the misconception that I'm an idiot, Denny Brooks. If I leave without you, you'll never show!"

I want to object but I know she's probably right. But there's no way I can just jump in a car and leave with her. I need time. I've been training my brain to go on autopilot for four years; I can't just flip the switch in a matter of hours.

The pressure of disappointing so many people is too much to absorb, but the clear evidence that I'm disappointing Rosie shoots right through my walls and pierces my heart. How the hell does she do that?

Brody treks back to the truck with a paddle and a tackle box and my words are carrying over the line before I can stop them. "Then don't leave."

I picture those arched eyebrows of hers drawing together. "What does that mean?"

"You still know how to bait a hook?"

Rosie must have been on the debate team in high school because, by the time we're done negotiating, I've agreed not only to go home for the surgery (*deep breaths, Brooks*) but to let Gwen tag along on what was supposed to be a cozy little fishing trip for two.

However, I've won an argument or two in my day as well, so I threw an overnight stay under the stars in as a condition of my cooperation. I think it's more than fair.

I know it sounds crazy, but sometimes I think the river has answers. And I know for a fact it has powers—how else could it carve through stone to form canyons and push its way ever forward? So what better place to prepare myself for the coming storm, and what better company than a woman who could probably make me agree to just about anything for a taste of her? Not that I'm making that part of the bargain, but I plan on doing my damn best to get her to share a sleeping bag with me—even if it's only to see her eyes light with fire as she shuts me down.

"Okay, I think we're all set." Brody adjusts his ballcap as he approaches our trio.

Rosie's mouth pops open in an O and I can almost hear the wheels turning in her brain. "Wait. You're joining us?"

See, what Rosie has clearly forgotten is that I play hardball. If Gwen's coming to chaperone, I'm providing a distraction for said chaperone—one that comes in the form of a six-foot-two former college ballplayer who thinks he knows how to flirt.

Brody smiles, taking no offense. "I got two tandem kayaks all rigged up." He throws out a double thumbs up that makes me mentally shake my head in embarrassment for him.

Gwen, who hasn't seemed all that jazzed to go on a fishing trip, suddenly brightens. Can I call 'em or what?

"Great! But I have to admit I've never been fishing before," she says, tucking her blond bob behind her ears.

Brody holds out an arm like he's offering to escort her to the damn prom. "Then you're riding with me. I can teach you everything I know."

I watch Gwen grin and feel a smug smile curve my lips until I turn to Rosie and remember to hide it. I'm too late.

"God, I never learn, do I?"

She shakes her head and stalks by me to the waiting truck, ponytail swinging. But that's okay, because she's wearing another pair of cutoffs and these have stars stitched into the back pockets, right over the cheeks of her sweet ass.

I'm gonna make the most of the next twenty-four hours if it kills me.

Brody drives us to a calmer section of the river where we can drift on the slow current and try our luck at catching dinner. While Brody packed the truck and loaded the kayaks, I borrowed his car to run back and grab a shower and any gear I needed. By the time I got back, Gwen and Rosie were pulling into the gravel lot along with the crew who was scheduled to work the rafting tours today.

Gwen and Rosie spend the drive alternately texting on their phones and chatting with Brody while I'm content to enjoy the view and the cadence of Rosie's voice. It's a touch deeper than I remember from way back, almost like it's the tiniest bit hoarse from not enough practice. It suits her, just like her new look and her new confidence. She's a completely different person than the last time I saw her at sixteen, yet she's somehow still the same. I suspect it's due to her heart being just as big as it always was. This thought makes me choke out a small laugh since pretty much all she's done since our reunion is give me shit. Not exactly the best reflection of a giving soul, but I haven't forgotten what brought her here in the first place. Brody shoots me a puzzled look but I shake my head and turn back to the window to watch the forest fly by.

"Okay, now give it a firm pull to set the hook."

Gwen jerks the rod up a bit too forcefully, but it seems to have worked regardless. "I got him!"

"Awesome! Now reel him in nice and steady." Rosie smiles as she instructs her friend.

I look over and scowl at Brody in the back of my kayak.

I should have anticipated Rosie conniving her way out of riding with me. A covert conversation must have been conducted on the ride over because, by the time Brody and I got the gear unloaded, Gwen and Rosie had chucked a tent, a cooler, and fishing gear in one of the kayaks and taken off. Brody and I stood gaping on the river's edge as they wiggled their fingers in mocking waves at us and laughed their asses off.

Rosie even clapped her hands together in what I assume was an imitation of me, yelling, "Better start paddling, ladies!"

As far as I'm concerned, she may have won this battle, but I'm still winning the war. Brody and I have the cooler with the drinks and fishing is thirsty work.

To that end, I make my voice loud enough to carry. "Hey, man, can you pass me a water?"

Brody cranks his reel while holding the rod in his other hand, completely oblivious to my game. "The cooler's right there. Can't you get one yourself?"

I scowl again and lower my voice. "Haven't you ever played wingman?" I throw a subtle chin to the girls' kayak and watch as comprehension dawns on Brody's face. He's lucky he's got decent looks or I'd be worried for him.

"Oh! You mean the ice-cold water from the cooler?!" he bellows, proving that his choice to pursue river guiding over acting was a sound one.

Brody tosses me a water and I don't miss Rosie's side-long glance. *That's right. You're gonna have to come closer if you want something to drink, Sunshine.*

But Rosie's not biting. Yet.

"That's it. Now pull back slowly and keep reeling him in." Rosie continues to instruct Gwen who's got her tongue trapped between her teeth as she pulls on the rod. A nice large-mouth bass jumps out of the water about ten feet from their kayak and Gwen yelps, making Rosie laugh and me forget all about our war. The sound is nothing short of magical as it echoes off the rock face behind us.

A minute later, Rosie is holding up the fish for us to admire, her smile bright and Gwen's triumphant.

"Woohoo!" Brody yells. "Looks like lunch!" To which Gwen frowns, dropping her eyes to the bass in Rosie's grip.

It flips its tail and her brow furrows. "*What?* We can't eat him! I already named him!"

Rosie throws back her head and laughs again before casually tossing the fish in the river while Brody and I watch in disbelief as our meal swims away.

"Bye, Rocky!" Gwen waves at the water, sending Rosie into another fit of laughter.

It seems the score is zero to two. I've got some catching up to do.

Chapter Six

It's ultimately nature—or, more accurately, the call of it—that offers me my chance to get Rosie alone. We pull out of the river at a low spot to take what Gwen declares a "water break," but she quickly disappears behind some trees. It's going on lunchtime, so I decide to put out some sandwiches I threw together when I went home earlier and take the opportunity to go for a swim. The fishing's been a tad slow, especially with Gwen and Rosie throwing all theirs back in the river, but between Brody and me we should have enough for dinner later.

I'm lounging on my back in the river when I catch sight of Rosie carefully picking her way over a few large rocks to take a dip herself. My heart gets its second dead stop of the day at the sight of her in a black and red one-piece swimsuit. This woman is about to make me the youngest guy I know to have a cardiologist on speed dial.

The front of the suit dips low while the shiny black material cups her full breasts and ties behind her neck. Red lacing crisscrosses over her cleavage to keep the suit in place, but it's more of a tease than anything. More lacing runs down the sides along her lush hips, leading to those long, tanned legs I can't get enough of. She's nothing short of stunning and I don't even pretend I'm not gawking.

When she notices me staring, she stops in her tracks. "What?" Her tone suggests she expects me to tell her a bear is standing behind her.

"You're beautiful." The words spill from my mouth and are nothing but the God's honest truth.

She blushes and it reminds me of when she was younger, but it's the *only* thing that's still childlike about her.

"Oh."

It seems I've accomplished the impossible and made Miss Rosina Carmichael speechless. That notion tugs a corner of my mouth upward and my look sends her jumping in the river—probably to cool her face.

I waste no time swimming in her direction.

She breaks through the water's surface a few feet from me and pulls in a gasp at the cool temperatures before running a hand over her face to clear the water from her eyes. She startles at my nearness when they open.

"Jesus, Denny. You scared the hell out of me." She squeezes the water from her long ponytail and I glance down to see her tightened nipples beneath the thin material of her suit. Granted, it's probably more to do with the cold, but I like to imagine I'm the cause.

When she sees where my eyes are focused, she looks down and gasps again before splashing me. "Pervert!"

I sputter and laugh at the same time. "Have you seen yourself in that suit?" I take a quick glance to the bank to make sure Brody's not getting an eyeful, but he's busy cleaning the fish for tonight's dinner and Gwen is working on a sandwich.

Rosie doesn't answer and, instead, ducks her head back under and swims across to the far side. An old tree has fallen into the river, creating a dam of sorts and allowing an almost still area of water to form.

"Don't get your foot caught!" She knows river safety and this is a slow area anyway, but the idea of her being trapped terrifies me nonetheless. My strokes bring me quickly to her side, but she's just floating on her back with her eyes closed and one hand resting on a branch to keep her in place. I'm unsure if she's aware of the spectacular view her position offers, but I'm not about to tell her —or complain. Frankly, I'm grateful for the water temperature as it's helping to keep my dick somewhat under control.

"I'm still trying to figure out your full motivation for this little trip." She surprises me by speaking without appearing to move a muscle. "I mean, I see it for the stall tactic it is, and I've been around men enough to know that you've set yourself some kind of challenge where I'm concerned."

I move closer until I'm looking down at her face. She opens her eyes, but she's not startled this time. Droplets of water cling to her lashes and pool in the indentation above her upper lip. I want to use my tongue to gather it to my mouth.

My eyes shift to hers and she holds my gaze. "But you have no right to play with me, Denny."

Her words make my breath catch. I mean, sure, we've both engaged in a bit of healthy competition over the last day, but I wouldn't play with her feelings in any way that might actually hurt her. I'm unsure what to say. The fact that she feels compelled to say this makes me think I've already done some serious damage in the past. But it was just a stupid crush. Wasn't it?

Rosie flicks her tongue to her upper lip and the water is gone. "I'm not a little girl anymore."

I want to tell her I've most definitely noticed that, but she continues before I can stick my foot in my mouth.

"And I'm over you. I have been for a long time."

Her words are a gut punch. I hadn't thought ahead any further than today, but the idea of living in a world where I have no place in Rosie Carmichael's heart suddenly sounds like my own personal hell.

"Rosie." It's all I can say.

"So don't think anything is happening between us today or any other day, Denny. I'm here to bring you home, and I won't sell my soul to do it."

She flips over to her stomach and swims away, leaving me staring at the fallen tree and the fading ripples of water she left in her wake.

Gwen sighs and sets her fork down. "This could have been Nemo."

I grin over my mouthful of delicious fried fish. Brody has outdone himself, and even Gwen couldn't resist eating the freshly-caught dinner, despite her declaration not to eat anything with a name.

"Nemo wasn't a trout. He was a clownfish." Brody tries to reassure her, but I think he's missing the point.

Gwen musters up a smile for him and I figure it's only a matter of time before those two sneak away to explore nature's wonders on their own.

I glance at Rosie who's sitting on a nearby rock, wrapped in my flannel shirt. It took ages to get her to accept my offer, but the cooling temperatures finally won out. Seeing her in my clothes makes my dick awaken yet again. My thoughts wander to her in my bed, wearing one of my t-shirts and nothing else. I repress a groan. This girl is leading me around by the cock without even trying.

I was afraid the serious nature of her announcement in the river earlier would put an end to any lightheartedness of the day, but as soon as we packed things up to resume kayaking, she was smiling and laughing again. She even agreed to ride with me for the duration, but I suspect it had more to do with allowing Gwen to hang out with Brody. I'd take what I could get, though.

It dawned on me that if I were going home, I had a shit-ton to catch up on—even if Lynn and Mama were likely to be the only ones to acknowledge me.

"So, Rosie, what are you studying?" I lift another bite of fish to my mouth.

Gwen giggles. "Did you just ask her what her major is?"

Brody guffaws and I see Rosie trying to suppress a grin as well.

Smooth as silk, Brooks. Nicely done.

"Shut up. It's a legitimate question." My defense is lame at best and everybody knows it, but Rosie takes pity on me.

"Biology."

"Seriously?" Damn, that's some genuinely complicated shit.

She shrugs. "I've always been good at science and I need a major that will get me a good job."

I'm pretty sure she doesn't mean anything by it, but I can't help thinking she might be referencing my choice of majoring in Environmental Education only to graduate and become a river guide. The pay may not be great, but the lifestyle can't be beat.

I really shouldn't be surprised that she's ambitious. She's never been one to give up on something she wants, that's for sure. But she did give up on me, didn't she? Never mind that I told her to. I set my plate aside, no longer hungry.

"Then maybe you can stop using all your free time doing your mending and sewing," Gwen chimes in. She rolls her eyes when I turn to her. "She never has any time to go out or do anything fun. Every time I call her, she's always at that damn sewing machine, slaving away for extra money."

My back goes straight at that. There's nothing wrong with working your way through school, but the way

Gwen's describing it, Rosie is missing out on the college experience entirely.

"Hey," Rosie cuts in, hugging my shirt around her. "It pays better than working food service, and besides, I like all that damn sewing." She grins at her friend.

"Nobody likes sewing that much. And I know for a fact that your mom told you to stop sending money home."

"Gwen!" Rosie tries to cut her off but she's too late to shove that cat back in the bag.

My eyes are glued to her face and her knitted brow. "Your parents in trouble?" I feel like even more of a shit-heel for not knowing one way or the other.

"No." Rosie gives her head a firm shake and produces a fake-ass smile for my benefit.

"Somebody's panties would be on fire," Gwen begins in a sing-song tone. "If she was wearing any, that is."

Rosie throws her plastic fork at Gwen, who ducks, but not fast enough. The fork gets stuck in her hair but she laughs it off and proudly wears it like it's a diamond tiara or some shit. The girl is nuts, but at least she's entertaining.

Rosie clearly thinks the money subject has been dropped, but there's no damn way I'm letting it go. I get up and scrape the remains of my dinner into the trash bag before turning to Rosie and lifting my chin. "Hey, you wanna help me find some more firewood?"

She sighs, understanding my motivation, and stands.

It's still light out and I've got the tree saw so we'll be able to pick up some wood from fallen branches, but I'm not concerned about the fire. I'm concerned about Rosie and what the hell is going on at home. Luca never said anything, but then again, why would he when I'd made it clear I didn't want to talk about Asheville or anyone residing there?

I can hear Rosie's footfalls behind me as I take us deeper into the canopy of trees. I don't turn around when I speak. "So, are you gonna tell me what happened?"

There's no need to look back to know she's scowling at me. "Not that it's any of your business, but my dad got laid off last year. He's been looking, but they'd have to leave Asheville for him to get anything comparable and they both refuse to leave."

That last part's not surprising. There's something about Asheville that sucks you in and makes it hard to break free. I know from experience.

"My mom keeps pretending everything is fine, but her salary is even shittier than what my dad's been able to pick up. I'm pretty sure they've blown through any retirement savings they had and they won't sell that death trap of a house."

This makes me smile just a bit. The Carmichael's house is full of what Adrina calls character—and by character she means floorboards that threaten to flip up and knock you out *Looney-Tunes*-style and the occasional wildlife that consider the dog door an invitation to move in.

But the dire financial situation kills any amusement I might feel at the memories. "So you've been sending them money." I glance back to see she's got her thumbnail trapped between her teeth and the image sends me back in time. She always did that when she was thinking on something. I'd forgotten that.

She releases her thumb and throws her arms out. "What else am I supposed to do? Luca and I are working as hard as we can, but he's got student loans to pay off. Mine won't come due until after I graduate, so I'm in a better position to help."

Fuck. I'm beginning to fully comprehend how well-deserved her greeting from yesterday was. Shithead, indeed.

"Why didn't you..." I trail off because there's no way to end that question that makes any sense. *Why didn't you call me* was what I was going to say, but the answer to that is already clear as this morning's sky.

She stops and I swear she stomps her foot like a ten-year-old. "How is this any of your business, anyway, Denny? You left." She stalks closer and I turn around to fully face her—just in time, it seems, because she shoves me in the chest. Hard. "YOU LEFT!"

I put my hands up and brace a foot behind me when I see a second shove coming. I won't try to stop her. It's well-deserved.

"I never took you as a coward, Denny Brooks." She's trying to make her voice cold, but I can see the tears in her eyes and hear the tremble in her voice.

I bring my hands in to cover hers where they lay flat against my t-shirt. My heart is beating like a humming-bird's wings and I'm sure she can feel it through my chest. I stroke the backs of her hands with my thumbs and slowly lean in until my forehead is resting against hers. She's breathing hard.

"You only saw what you wanted to see when you looked at me. I meant it when I said I was no good for you." My words try to catch in my throat but I push them out.

I continue the rhythmic movement of my thumbs against her smooth skin and inhale the scent of her. She still smells like sunshine against the river—a scent that's hard to explain unless you live it like I do.

Rosie sniffles. "I'm pretty sure you cited some state laws and tried to embarrass the shit out of me, but close enough."

I choke out a strangled laugh. "Yeah, I guess I did."

Chapter Seven

The third time Rosie Carmichael tried to kiss me was the week after my dad's funeral.

I'd timed my escape perfectly; Carter was back in D.C., Cash was at work, Lynn was at a friend's house, Mama was out running errands, and who the hell knew where Miller was.

I'd just graduated, so I was back in Asheville when the whole clusterfuck went down and our world imploded. My plan had been to work my regular summer job doing rafting tours in town until my new job as a Conservation Field Supervisor started in a couple months, but plans change. I was escaping to Colorado instead.

The house felt so strange without my dad in it. His ugly-ass Crocs waited by the back door for him to slip his feet in them and the den still smelled like his favorite black coffee. It made no sense.

I hefted my backpack on my shoulder and opened the door, only to find Rosina standing on the porch, thumbnail clenched between her teeth and hair pulled back in a braid. Her brow was furrowed when she looked up at me and released her thumb.

"I saw you packing your car."

Dammit. Why hadn't I considered my little watch dog?

"Yup." The less I said, the better.

She followed me as I walked to my beat-up Ford and opened the back door to throw in my pack. She'd turned gangly in the last few years, her legs growing faster than the rest of her body could keep up. And she'd started making her own clothes, most of which were downright confusing with their mixed patterns and colors that threatened to burn your eyes. Today's shirt was an oversized bright yellow abomination that reminded me of PacMan.

"Where are you going?"

I shut the door and leaned against it with a sigh. "I just need to get away for a while, Rosie. It's no big deal."

"But." She swallowed hard. "Your mama. Lynn."

Shit. I didn't need her reminding me. I pushed off the door and scoffed. "You're too young to understand."

She got up in my face, her voice stronger than I'd ever heard it. "Just because I'm younger than you doesn't mean I'm *too young*. I'm sixteen, Denny."

I rolled my eyes. "Fine, then. How about *it's none of your business*, then?"

Her eyes narrowed, pulling down her bushy eyebrows. "It is too my business."

I laughed at that, making her mouth go tight. "How do you figure?"

Her chest expanded with a deep inhale as she looked to

the side. "Because I love you, Denny Brooks." And then she was all up in my face and rising to her toes, her pursed lips on a direct path to mine.

I got my hand up just in time and her mouth brushed against my palm before I stepped back. "For Christ's sake, Rosie. You've got to stop doing that!"

She dropped back on her heels and her mouth twisted. Shit, she was gonna cry.

I sighed. "I'm no good for you. I'm no good for anybody." She sniffled as I continued, "And you only think you love me, but you'll see I'm right."

This wasn't helping so I switched tactics. "And, besides, there are laws about these things." I figured her goody-two-shoes nature would at least respect the rule of law if nothing else. "Men want things you're not ready to give, so don't go chasing them. A grown man can't date a teenager. It's just... wrong. In so many ways."

This made her blush, but she looked back up at me, tears swimming in her eyes. "Please, Denny, don't go. Even if you don't love me back, please stay. We can't lose you too."

My skin caught fire at her words and flashes of white danced in my vision. Her final comment was a reflection of all my fears. *We can't lose you too.* I was done with loss. With worry. With grief. I couldn't take another blow. So I was leaving.

I opened the front door of my car and climbed in on autopilot. "I'm sorry," I said before closing it and turning my key in the ignition. I pulled out of the drive and tried not to glance at the rearview mirror, but it was out of my control. The last thing I saw of home was Rosie sinking to her knees in my driveway, her yellow shirt engulfing her whole body and her face buried in her hands.

My forehead is still pressed to Rosie's and her breathing has calmed, so I try to lighten the mood. "So, I assume you're sewing skills have improved since people are actually paying for your stuff now?"

She draws her head back and looks up at me. "I've always been an excellent sewer, for your information."

I smile. "Then maybe it's your taste that's improved because I remember some of the shit you used to wear."

Her jaw drops and she tries to pull her hands back, but I keep my grip on them. "I was just ahead of my time." She looks down at the checked flannel shirt. "Besides, you're one to talk when it comes to fashion."

"Hey, I saw that exact same pattern on some movie star the other day on TV."

Rosie raises a brow. "I can guaran-damn-tee you she hasn't owned that shirt for ten years like this one. It's sheer coincidence and nothing more."

She's being playful again, which was my entire goal. "So why didn't you go into fashion design or something?"

Her responding laugh makes my stomach dip. "Because I didn't want to work at McDonald's."

I want to object, but I can't. "Touché." She's talking like a realist, but she's supposed to still be a dreamer.

"Are we getting some firewood or what?" When she pulls her hands back this time, I let them go. She's either forgiven me for something or she's chosen to set it aside.

"Sure. I'll even let you wield the tree saw."

This wins me a grin and I let her lead the way through the trees.

By the time we get back from fetching firewood, Gwen and Brody have cleaned up and retreated to one of the tents, leaving Rosie and me to share the other one. Given the events of the afternoon, I'm no longer intent on trying anything on with her—not that I don't want to lick her body from head to toe, but she's made herself clear and I understand the importance of respecting that. I don't ever want to hurt her again, if only to avoid seeing the shine of tears in her sky-blue eyes. The only playing I plan on doing is the kind where our clothes stay on.

To that end, I unpack a deck of cards and tell Rosie to shuffle while I lay a couple new pieces of wood on the dwindling fire. We use a flat rock as our playing surface and Rosie turns on some music on her phone to drown out the hushed conversation coming from Gwen and Brody's tent.

"Gin?" She asks when I settle across from her.

"You sure you wanna go there? It's my specialty."

She tilts her head and throws a card down in front of me. "Well, isn't that a coincidence. It just so happens to be mine too."

Her grin is naughty as she continues to deal. "Game on."

I win the first round by a small margin and Rosie blows me away on the second, claiming overall victory, despite my objection.

My water bottle thuds as it lands on the rock. "That's not how it works. When the Panthers win, it doesn't matter if it's by one point or forty, it still counts as a W."

She gathers the cards and stacks them. "That may be true, but I'm talking about rankings. Assuming an equal record, if the Panthers win a game by forty and the Falcons play a game the same day and win by one, the Panthers are definitely going to rank ahead of the Falcons."

"Wait. Am I the Falcons in your little scenario? 'Cuz that's not funny."

She shrugs and taps the deck on the rock to straighten the cards. "Hey, you're the one who lives in Georgia." She glances around meaningfully at our surroundings, knowing full well the Chattooga runs along the border of South Carolina and Georgia.

"I live on the South Carolina side, thank you very much." My tiny rental cabin is nestled in the woods firmly rooted in Carolina soil.

"Fine, if you're going to whine about it, let's play a tie-breaker." She moves to shuffle the cards again but I put a hand out to stop her.

"All right, but not Gin. I have something else in mind for a tie-breaker."

I don't know what possesses me. Maybe it's nostalgia or maybe it's just the need to get away from whatever may or may not be going on in the tent fifteen feet away. Whatever it is has me leading Rosie by the hand along a low rocky outcropping and up a set of stacked boulders to a path that starts on the raised section of ground above. We've both got headlights on, but it's still a bit foolish of me to take her on this trek in the dark.

Brody and I know this area like the backs of our hands, though, which is how we knew the best spot to stop for the night. We'd planned on surprising the girls with this little outing in the morning, but I can't seem to wait until then.

"Are there mountain lions out here?" Rosie asks from behind me. The path is too narrow for us to walk side-by-side.

I glance back at her with a grin but get blinded by her headlight. "Ow." I shield my eyes. "No, there are no mountain lions out here."

I hear her exhale of relief and resume walking. "But you might want to keep an eye out for black bears. Why do you think we hang all the food and garbage in a tree?"

Her chest is plastered to my back before I even finish my question. I bust out laughing.

She huffs and I can feel her warm breath on my skin. "Shut up."

We practically frog walk the rest of the way, but I don't mind because it means the warmth of her full breasts presses against my back with each step. I'm almost disappointed when we reach our destination and come to a stop.

"Well, here we are."

Rosie's headlight illuminates the space as she looks around. "What is this?"

I take her hand and pull her with me onto the expanse of smooth rock before us until we're only a couple feet from the edge. "Stand still," I command as I lean forward and point my headlight straight down into the water below.

"Oh my God." I can't tell if she's scared or just plain surprised.

Now, normally, jumping twenty feet into a pool of water in the dark is about as smart as trying to shave your balls with a kitchen knife, but this is part of my stomping grounds. I know every rock and ripple in this swimming hole, so I can guarantee Rosie's safety.

"Go on, girl. Strip." I say as I pull off my shirt.

She tries to look appalled but ruins it by laughing. "It's cold."

"Then you best get movin'." I pull off everything but my board shorts before she's even started on the buttons of the flannel shirt.

She looks down to the water and then back at me again, this time adjusting her light so it doesn't shine right in my face. "And how exactly is this a tie-breaker?"

I waggle my brows and say, "Last one in is the loser," before letting out a whoop and launching myself over the side.

It takes her a minute, but Rosie finally jumps down with a screech that has me laughing. She surfaces, her headlight still glowing. Just about everything I own is waterproof, including the lights.

"It's frickin' freezing!" she hollers as she wipes her face.

"Oh, come on. You can take it." I tread water and watch her rub her lips together. "Remember that time you tagged along with Luca and me to Sliding Rock?"

That prompts a smile. "Yeah. My mom forced you guys to take me and neither one of you talked to me the whole ride there."

"We were sixteen. We were jackasses." I remember purposely ignoring her as she chatted on about some TV show the whole way. Luca and I were sure she'd chicken out once she saw the huge sixty-foot boulder with cold mountain water running like the devil down into the chilly pool below.

"I still love that place." Her smile grows wider and it's dazzling.

I laugh. "And you're complaining about this water? It's got to be at least twenty degrees warmer!"

Instead of responding, she splashes me in the face. Okay, so it is a bit chilly, but my body is feeling nothing but warmth at her proximity. I wipe the water from my eyes and, quick as lightning, grab her and pretend I'm going to dunk her.

"No! Stop!" She's laughing and gripping onto my shoulders for purchase.

I ease my grip and slide my hands down from her waist to her hips. My fingers flex on her skin of their own accord and she stops laughing. Water from her hair drips down either side of her face and I can feel her own fingers flex on the bare skin of my shoulders. Her eyes search my face and I have not one clue what she's looking for.

"Rosie."

She finally drops her gaze to my lips. "This doesn't mean anything, you got that?" she asks before she brings her lips to mine.

Chapter Eight

Kissing while treading water is more difficult than it sounds, but I'm determined to master it if it takes my last breath to do so. The kiss is hot and wet, the latter having nothing at all to do with the water surrounding us. Rosie caresses my tongue with hers and lets out a little moan when I squeeze her hips in my palms.

But I'm letting her control the kiss while I take care of keeping us above water. If I thought she would be shy about the kiss, I'm dead wrong because, before I know it, her hands are exploring my shoulders and back and she's digging her nails in, which makes my dick hard as a rock. Then she's slanting her mouth and wrapping her thighs around my hips. I groan and scrape my teeth along her lips as she presses her center against the length of my cock.

Fuck. Me.

We've got to get out of this water before my southern-most brain decides getting inside Rosie is worth drowning the both of us. My mouth grazes down to her chin and along her jaw to her ear.

"Fuck, Rosie. You're so fuckin' hot." My words are flowing free with no filter at all. "I knew you'd be the best thing I ever tasted."

She tries to pull my mouth back to hers as she rocks firmly against me, the pressure turning me stupid. I forget to move my feet for a second and we're both sinking. As soon as my nose goes under, I snap out of it and push Rosie up. Her legs release me so she can tread water on her own, and I bring my head above water to catch a breath.

"Shit. Sorry." I hold onto her and shake my head hard since I don't have a free hand to wipe my face.

She's panting and holding onto my biceps. "We should get out." She lets go and swims for the edge, her headlight guiding the way. I realize then that I lost my headlight somewhere in the midst of our kiss and I don't see any sign of it. I keep my eye on Rosie's ass and follow her to the water's edge. We pull ourselves out at the base of the arranged rock steps that lead back to the top. I'm still hard and there's no sign that's changing anytime soon, so I don't bother trying to hide the tent in my board shorts.

Rosie glances down and then darts her eyes to the side. I laugh at the contrast between her sudden reticence and the boldness of the girl who undoubtedly left scratch marks on my back in the water out there.

"Hey, it's not rude to stare when you're the one responsible for it."

The corner of her mouth twitches and she squeezes the water from her hair. "I'll take that into consideration." She turns to me again, but her eyes are on my face. "What happened to your light?"

I shrug and can't help my grin. "A Siren ripped it off and chucked it into the depths while she had her dirty way with me."

"I did not!"

"Who said I meant you?" I run my hands over my own hair and brush as much water as I can from my chest and arms.

She shakes her head and goes for the first step. "Whatever you say, Captain." She glances back, her headlight shining on my feet. "But if you want to find your way to the top, you'd better be close behind."

That's an invitation I'd be an idiot to refuse.

We get to the top and I'm deserving of an award for keeping my hands off her hips and ass on the way up. The way her swimsuit clings and cuts up the sides has my mouth watering and my hands practically shaking.

But Rosie goes straight for my flannel shirt, wrapping it around herself without bothering with her t-shirt from earlier. The cutoffs go on next so I'm left with only her long legs and gorgeous face to ogle.

We're both silent as we finish dressing over our wet suits, but once we have our shoes back on, Rosie breaks the silence.

"Hey. Like I said, please don't read anything into that. It was a one-time thing. Nothing more."

The me from two days ago would have been the one to say exactly those words to a girl I kissed—or slept with, probably. But I'm no longer the me from two days ago.

Whoever I am, though, I know I don't deserve Rosie—or her kisses. So I just nod my understanding and gesture for her to lead the way back to the campsite.

Again, I'm surprised that things aren't more awkward. We chat about mundane shit on the way back and take turns changing into dry clothes in the tent. I assume Gwen and Brody have dozed off because there's little sound coming from their tent—not that I'm listening all that closely.

Rosie and I settle into our separate sleeping bags, whispering about the last time our families went camping together. So much of my history is entwined with hers, yet I never really thought about it until now. I always considered it to be about Luca and me, but Rosie was an important part of it as well, even if I never really treated her as such.

Yeah, she was right to cut me off before I got any crazy ideas. I wonder briefly how badly Luca would beat me if he knew I touched his little sister, but I know no matter how brutal the beating, it was totally worth it.

"What are you smiling about?" Rosie asks, both her hands tucked under her cheek like a child as she lays against the pack she's using as a pillow.

I shake my head. "Nothing."

She smiles back and then yawns.

"I had a great time today," I tell her.

"Me too." She blinks a few times and I can see the day's activities catching up to her. "'Night, Denny."

"'Night, Sunshine." Because she is. Rosie is the sun. It should be all of us orbiting her instead of the other way around. She's not the pest circling me and my ever-important world. She's the light, the drawing force that pulls us in and keeps our worlds from hurtling into oblivion.

Rosie giggles and I reach over to cover her mouth, but it doesn't work for shit because the sound passes right through my fingers at her next eruption of hilarity. Not that I can really blame her.

The noises coming from the next tent over are straight out of a National Geographic video—before they started editing out all the mating rituals.

I have no idea what time it is, but we both woke up about ten minutes ago to what sounded like a pig searching for truffles. Our heads simultaneously snapped toward each other's, our eyes darting around as we tried to determine the source.

It became all too obvious when a voice undoubtedly belonging to Gwen cried out, "Right there!" and then, "Motherfuuuuuu!" and then, "Omigod, omigod, omigod, omigod!" before letting out a screech that could likely be heard from Atlanta.

That was when the giggling started.

It got worse when Brody's noises grew louder. The truffle hunting switched to more of a grunting bull and then a full-on wolf howl reminiscent of every B-movie featuring a werewolf. I honestly don't know if I'll ever be able to look the guy in the eye again.

"Shhhh." I go for a good seal this time and Rosie's breath puffs against my palm as her entire body shakes.

"Mimompombr." Her mumble is indecipherable, so she tries prying my hand away.

"You have to promise to stay quiet," I whisper. When she nods, I let go.

Her effort to keep from laughing ends in a snort, the sound of which sends my head back to my pack in silent laughter while she covers her mouth again. We both breathe for a moment until she's calm enough to speak.

"What the fuck are they doing? Is it just the two of them in there or is Brody into bestiality?"

I throw my arm over my face, trying like hell not to laugh out loud.

"I mean, at least Gwen is speaking English. Kind of."

As if to prove Rosie's point, a quick succession of "Oh! Oh! Oh!" resounds from the tent next door.

I get ahold of myself enough to whisper. "I think they're engaging in cunnilingus. If I'm not mistaken, that's Latin for eating clams."

A low growl comes next and Gwen literally squeaks at whatever the fuck Brody is doing to her.

Rosie whispers back on a stuttered laugh, "I thought it was French for painting the kitty."

We throw around a few more colorful descriptions until we hear what must be the grand finale, based on the sheer number of filthy curses hurled by Gwen and the King Kong grunts coming from Brody.

Rosie covers her mouth and snorts again.

I lose my shit and laugh out loud.

Brody finally regains his ability to speak, uttering one single word. "Dayum."

Gwen sighs audibly, following that with, "Your turn."

"No!" Rosie and I yell at the exact same time.

Chapter Nine

The next morning, Brody has the good grace to look at least a little chagrined, but Gwen? Nope.

"God, it's so beautiful out here, isn't it?" She flashes a bright smile to Rosie and me while she tucks her hair behind her ear and pours herself a cup of coffee.

Rosie groans from her perch on a rock, both hands wrapped around her own cup of coffee. "Ask me again when I get another ten hours of sleep."

The implication sails completely over Gwen's head as she casually pats Rosie on the shoulder and walks over to Brody, who's taking down their tent.

Rosie's mouth splits in a giant yawn that makes me grin. She's wearing my flannel again, something that makes me ridiculously pleased.

"How far back do you and Gwen go?" I ask her as I douse the fire and pick up my shovel to add some soil.

She sips her coffee and lets out a grateful-sounding

sigh. "Really just high school. They moved to town right before our senior year and she and I just clicked, I guess." Her lips curve in a smile brought on by what I assume is some memory or other. "She tried to get me to go to SCUW with her but she's learned to adjust to texting me every five minutes instead of being roomies. And she picks me up for visits now and then—like this week."

I want to ask why she doesn't drive herself, but I can guess the answer. The girl doesn't have a damn car. And it's not hard to understand why she stayed closer to home for college; in-state tuition is a lot cheaper, and I know her heart's in North Carolina.

"Well, if you ask me, App State sounds way more fun than SCUW." Although the bikini ratio *is* lower. I don't mention that, though, because one-piece swimsuits with red lacing have recently become my clear preference.

But Rosie's smile drops and she turns her head like she's trying to hide it from me.

"You don't like App?" I poke the logs absently while I watch her.

I can see her chest expand with an inhale before she turns back to me. "I'm transferring to UNCA so I can live at home."

Fuck.

"Rosie... hell, you shouldn't have to do that." I ditch the shovel and step closer. "Shove over a bit." She slides her ass a few inches to the side and I join her on her rock, our sides flush against one another.

She stares down into her coffee. "It's no big deal,

Denny. A degree is a degree, no matter where it comes from. And UNCA is a good school too."

I'm in awe of this woman. She doesn't have a selfish bone in her body.

I'm such an asshole.

"I wouldn't go that far." Rosie turns to me and a hint of a smile is back.

"I said that out loud, didn't I?" Best to own it, I guess.

This makes her laugh and, as usual, it goes right to my chest.

She leans into me and I want to put my arm around her, pull her to me. "Hey, you're going home for the surgery, so that's a start. Don't be too hard on yourself."

My eyebrows reach for my hairline. "This is a change of tune since yesterday."

She shrugs. "What can I say? You're growing on me." She gives me a healthy shoulder bump.

I shake my head in wonder. "You are nothing short of amazing, Rosie Carmichael."

She coughs out an uncomfortable laugh and lifts her coffee mug again. "Whatever."

"Not *whatever*. I don't think I could ever be half as strong as you."

She swallows and turns to me again. "You never know till you try." Her eyebrow lifts and she stands. "And as long as I'm dropping clichés, here's another one: You only live once."

With that, she walks away. It doesn't occur to me until a minute later that she has my brain working so hard I forgot to stare at her ass as she left.

"Now, I know there's no chance this is a butt dial!"

I cough out a laugh. "It occurred to me that you're a bit spoiled if Mama let you keep your phone while you're grounded."

Lynn huffs into the phone. "I had to promise not to take any calls or texts from Ben."

"And she trusts you?" I pace to the other side of the wide rock I'm standing on.

"Hey! I'm a very trustworthy person. I can keep a secret better than anyone out there—something you should know by the fact that your phone hasn't been ringing off the hook since you called me. Please take note." Lynn's voice is full of attitude and I can only imagine what she puts our mother through.

"Taken." But her ability to keep a secret is something I already knew, which is why I chose Lynn to reach out to in the first place. "How's Mama?"

Lynn sighs. "Same as ever. She keeps trying to climb the stairs and acts all innocent every time I catch her."

"Sounds about right." I pace back to the other side.

"Carter drove in last night, though, and he's got her sequestered to the first floor."

It seems everybody is playing their designated role. As the oldest, Carter has always deemed himself the boss of every damn person and every damn thing.

Lynn's next words surprise the shit out of me. "So, how's Rosie?"

I'm speechless for a second, so Lynn continues, "Just because I'm grounded doesn't mean Adrina's not all up in my business."

I run a hand over my face and go for casual. "She's good."

Lynn cackles and I have to pull the phone from my ear for a second so my eardrum doesn't burst. "I would have paid good money to see your face when she showed up."

"Well. It was a surprise."

"I'll say! I bet your eyeballs fell straight outta your head." Another cackle breaks through the line and this one sounds downright evil.

"Can we please not talk about this?" I scrub a hand over my hair this time. I am not talking about hot women with my baby sister.

"You don't need to tell me shit. I already know exactly what's going on." Lynn has far too much sass for my comfort level.

I'm suddenly very glad I stepped far enough away from the campsite not to be overheard. "You don't know anything, Lynnie. Don't you need to be at school or something?" Despite the fact that I was the one to call, I'm dying for this little chat to end.

"No. I have free study first period so I've still got at least forty minutes." She sounds way too pleased. "And I do, in fact, know a hell of a lot. Adrina said Rosie is still there—even though she was supposed to be home yesterday morning."

Well, shit.

Again, she takes my silence as an invitation to go on.

"It's about time you started noticing Rosie, although I kind of hope she's giving you a run for your money." Lynn laughs, the evil streak still loud and clear.

I stop my pacing and stare at the rock wall across the river. "What's that supposed to mean?"

"Oh, please. That girl's been in love with you since I can remember, and you've been pushing her away her whole damn life."

I shake my head. "Does Mama know you cuss so much?"

She ignores me. "But from what Adrina said, it sounds like you're the one doing the chasing now. Fishing trip, Denny? A little desperate, don't you think?"

Who is this girl and what did she do with my baby sister? "Enough with the sass! This is none of your business, Loretta Lynn!!"

She gasps. "How dare you?" Then she huffs. "*Denver!*"

I growl. Although, I have to admit Lynn faired worse than I did in our mother's crazy Country-star name pool. Carter, Cash, and Miller got away easy compared to Lynn and me, though. I spent the whole third grade being called Omelet.

"I hope you're not being this rude to Rosie or she might decide to fall right out of love with you."

I'm tempted to tell her that ship has already sailed, but I don't want to encourage any more of this line of conversation. Instead, I switch to the original reason for my call to divert her attention.

"Well, you just wait until tonight and I can be rude right to your face."

There's nothing but silence on Lynn's end for a full five seconds and then she lets out a loud whoop that has my ear ringing. "Oh my God! She did it!"

I know she's talking about Rosie. "Well, she can be a bit... persuasive."

Lynn giggles. "I'll bet."

"Hey! I didn't mean it like that! Dammit, Lynn!"

"Whatever. I don't even care—I'm just so happy you're coming home!! Mama's not gonna believe her eyes! What time are you getting here?"

I close my eyes so I can think. "I'm not sure yet. We're still on the water." I figure we only have an hour's ride till we reach the boathouse, but there's still a lot to do—retrieve the truck, get the kayaks and gear put away, pack a bag, convince someone to switch shifts with me for a few days. And Brody still wants to take Gwen to the swimming hole. "I'd plan on dinner time, but don't tell Mama. I want it to be a surprise."

"My lips are sealed. Eeek! I'm so excited!"

I'm smiling ear to ear when I hang up the phone and it takes me a second to realize Rosie's watching me from her position by one of the kayaks. I purposely stepped away for some privacy, but I don't know how long she's been looking. I meet her eyes, and even from this distance, I can see that hers have gone soft. I hold her gaze, not wanting to miss a second of that look. I remember it. Those are the same eyes that fell on me time and time again when we were growing up. They hold promise, hope, affection—all the things I took for granted.

Is it possible that part of Rosie's heart still belongs to

me? And, if it does, what should I do? Because, for the first time in my life, I'm determined to put her feelings first.

Chapter Ten

I don't get long to enjoy Rosie's gaze before she's pulled aside by Gwen to look at something in the water.

I traverse the rocks back to the campsite and I swear my chest is swelling and my heart is racing double-time. I've felt more alive in the last twenty-four hours than the last four years combined, and there's one person I owe that to. The thing about running away from everything you love is that you forget what it feels like for your heart to be full. And it's fucking exhilarating. I was too focused on the grief to remember the other side of the coin.

The women have found an old Nerf ball wedged between some rocks and they're tossing it back and forth while I load the last of the things into the kayaks. The plan is to go to the swimming hole and then come back to grab the kayaks and head downstream to the boathouse. We're all wearing our swimsuits and Brody can't seem to keep his eyes off all the exposed skin Gwen's bikini affords. The dude has it bad, but I can't really talk.

When I look back at the girls, I see Rosie wading in the water, heading to the middle of the river where the water flows to either side of a group of large rocks. I'm watching her body move, as usual, so I almost get hit in the head when Gwen yells, "Catch, Denny!" I turn just in time to snatch the ball from the air. I toss is back and look to Rosie again. She has her hair down this morning and it cascades down her back in a dark flow of silk, making me imagine how it would look spread across my pillow.

Shit. I need to stop my thoughts before I get hard again. But I'm coming to realize I don't want to say goodbye to Rosie. Not today, not after my mama's surgery, not anytime in the foreseeable future.

Maybe it's time to suck it up and go home for good. Rosie and I can get something going for real and I can work at one of the outfitters nearby. Then I can try making up for all the lost time and start rebuilding my life again. Maybe Rosie is right and I'm stronger than I think.

"Yo! Romeo!" Gwen shouts and I turn again to catch her perfect spiral. Not bad at all, but I could do without the nickname.

"Hey, Denny!" Rosie shouts from the river. She's made her way up onto one of the boulders protruding from the water. A corner of my mouth ticks up when she waves, sending me that wide grin, her long dark hair flying around her in the breeze.

She's a goddess.

"I'm open!" She mimics a fake to the left and then throws both hands up.

And a complete nut.

I'm fairly certain we're about to lose the ball to the current, but I throw it anyway. Rosie shifts her weight and leans forward to catch it, almost losing her balance and falling into the river before she rights herself. My heart skips a beat and I feel my mouth turn down. She's not wearing a vest.

I forget the kayak and the game of catch as I straighten. "That's enough! Get down before you fall, Rosie!"

"I'm fine!" She tosses the ball from one hand to the other as if to prove it to me. Then she extends her arm back to toss it to Gwen, who's farther back than me. "Gwen! Catch!" She hurls the ball into the air, but the force of her movement sends her left shoe slipping forward. I watch in horror as the next moment plays out in what feels like slow motion.

People always say that, and I never believed it was true that time could slow down, but it does.

Rosie's foot slips out from beneath her and she's falling backward off the highest boulder. I see both shoes in the air and then nothing. She's gone.

"Rosie!" I shout and I'm in the water, swimming like Jaws himself is chasing me. I'm the human embodiment of terror, urgency, and speed.

I can hear Gwen yelling for Brody but my only focus is getting to Rosie. I hurl myself onto the rocks and scrabble to the other side, praying with everything in me that I'll find her on her back laughing at herself. But I don't. The current runs past the boulder there and the water is several feet deep.

"Denny! There!" I hear Brody shout and I look to see

him pointing several yards downstream. He's in his kayak paddling like mad in that direction. I'll never beat him there and I'm so thankful for his presence of mind to take the kayak instead of swimming like me. I dive back in and stroke downstream, my muscles burning and my breath coming in panicked waves when my mouth breaks the surface. Brody throws his paddle down and jumps in the water. I can't see what's going on at first but then I see her! Brody's holding Rosie out of the water and dragging her back across to the level bank on the side we came from.

I change direction and am torn between the need to keep my eye on Rosie and the need to swim as fast as possible to reach her.

I see Gwen paddling the other kayak toward Brody and a brief glance shows all three of them have reached the bank. I finally get there and sprint to where they are. Gwen has a phone to her ear as she drags the kayak on land. Brody is bent over Rosie, his ear to her mouth and nose checking for breathing. I make every promise I can possibly think of to God. I'll do anything as long as he lets Rosie be okay.

Brody's head comes up and his mouth is tight with worry. "She's breathing."

I exhale a breath I didn't realize I was holding and drop to my knees.

Just then, the most beautiful sound in the world hits my ears.

"Ow."

We all look down at Rosie. Her eyes are still closed but her hand is reaching for her head.

"Don't move," Brody instructs.

She opens her eyes and I crawl closer until I'm right beside her.

"Believe me, I don't want to," she croaks, making Gwen let out a relieved laugh.

"She's awake. Oh, thank God. She's awake. I think she hit her head." Gwen is talking into the phone, I assume to 9-1-1.

"I need to assess your injuries." Brody goes right into the training we've all received, but I'm fucking useless. All I can do is hold Rosie's hand and bend to press my lips to her palm. She's going to be okay. She *has* to be okay.

"Oh, tesoro mio!" Adrina bursts through the ER room door and immediately floods the entire space with her personality. She only has eyes for Rosie, who's lying in the bed with a bandage on her head and a blanket pulled up to her chest.

An endless flow of Italian streams from Adrina's red-lipsticked mouth, punctuated by Rosie's occasional, "Mamma," which Adrina completely ignores.

I slink outside and walk back to the waiting room to give them some privacy, even though I can't understand a single word Rosie's mom is saying. She goes into full-on Italian mode when she's stressed out, something I'd forgotten.

Gwen and Brody lean into one another in hushed

conversation, so I manage to sneak by without being noticed. I need fresh air and room to breathe.

In those moments when I thought Rosie might be dead, I wanted to die with her. I knew to my bones I couldn't suffer another death. I'd only opened myself up for a day or two and I could feel the pain begin to slice through me like a rusty knife, tearing open a ragged wound that had no chance of healing.

The bone-deep relief at hearing her voice and watching her eyes open pushed my desperation aside, only leaving room for getting Rosie to safety and ensuring she didn't have any hidden injuries. There was the gash on the back of her head, and a likely concussion, but other than that she seemed to be okay. She didn't even object when they shaved a section of her hair to stitch her up. Just like I knew, she's strong as steel.

But, while Rosie's spirit and strength carried her through the crazy rescue and transport to the hospital, as well as the treatment and head shaving, whatever strength I might have found conversely faded.

I've been sitting in the ER room as they wheel her in and out for x-rays, stitches, and whatever the hell else. My encouraging smile hasn't wavered in her presence since we arrived and I demanded to be allowed in with her. But, just like right now, when I'm alone the smile fades and reality seeps in.

This is exactly why I left home. If you don't know what's going on, if you don't see the faces of the people you love, you can insert a distance that keeps you from worrying—that keeps you safe from a broken fucking heart.

I can't ever fully erase the memory of my mother's eyes when she told us Dad had passed. It was unfathomable. He'd gone in for routine surgery and never come out. He was the cornerstone of our family, and without him, it wouldn't work. It couldn't.

The glass double doors part and my steps pick up speed. I need to get out of here. I need to put distance between Rosie and me, and I need to do it fast. I quickly form a plan. I'll call an Uber and pack my shit when I get home. I can be on the road within a couple hours and on my way to... wherever the fuck I can be alone. All I need is a river and the sun above.

Who wants to live their life constantly worrying and waiting for the other shoe to drop? Not me, that's for damn sure.

"It's reassuring to know you haven't changed."

The words stop me so abruptly I almost fall on my face.

There's no need to turn to know exactly what I'll see. What is it with the women from my past sneaking up on me?

"My God, you're a sight for sore eyes, Denny."

My chest squeezes when I try to breathe normally. Thank goodness I'm at a hospital in case it's the real thing this time. I try for another breath, but it's more of a wheeze. I close my eyes and concentrate on oxygen. In. Out. In. Out. It's getting easier.

I blink my eyes open and there she is, standing right in front of me. Well, sort of. She's got one foot on the ground, the other leg bent as she supports herself with crutches. Her hair is lighter and shorter than the last time I saw her, but her face is exactly the same.

My vision blurs, and for a second I think I'm passing out again, but I realize it's tears. I'm twenty-six fucking years old and the sight of my mama is making me cry like some little kid.

"Oh, baby." Her hand comes up to my cheek and one of her crutches drops to the ground.

I wipe my eyes with a thumb and forefinger and bend to get her crutch, glancing around for a place to sit. "Come on, Mama." I stand again and lead her to a bench she must have been sitting on while she waited for me to run. Just like she knew I would.

I get her settled, and her wince of pain doesn't escape me.

"What are you doing here?" I take a seat next to her on the wood surface.

"Stopping you from making a big mistake."

Well, she's always been a bit blunt, so I shouldn't be surprised. I don't respond because I know I don't have to.

My cell phone rings in my pocket and I ignore it.

Mama nods. "That'll be Lynn, I expect."

I pull the phone out and, sure enough, Lynn's number lights the screen. I press accept and lift it to my ear.

"Please tell me Mama's there."

I look over at my mother again. "Sitting right next to me, in fact."

"That sneaky little... let me talk to her."

I extend the phone to Mama but she shakes her head. "Tell her I'll call her later."

"Mama says—"

"I heard her," Lynn cuts me off. "She said she was going to dinner with Mrs. Nguyen and then never came home!"

A reluctant smile pulls at my lips. "Well, then I'd say Mrs. Nguyen has officially been stood up."

"Very funny." I try to picture Lynn's face, but all I can see is the one belonging to a thirteen-year-old. "Fine, you talk to her, but tell her to pick up her phone when I call her next time!"

Lynn hangs up and I look at Mama.

"What in the world has happened to Lynn? She's a regular sassafrass."

Mama rolls her eyes. "You don't need to tell me. She's comin' into her own, that's all, though."

"If you say so." I shove my phone back in my pocket, not wanting to return to the original topic but knowing I can't just get up and walk away—for countless reasons.

"So, Denny." She grabs my hand in one of hers and uses her other to pat it, just like she's done since I was a kid. "I reckon four years is enough time, don't you?"

Shit. I can't do this with her.

She gives my hand another pat. "I gave it to you because I know you needed some time. We all grieve differently, and I honestly wasn't all that surprised, to tell you the truth. You've always felt things... deeper than your brothers and sister." I open my mouth to protest, but she cuts me off. "Don't get me wrong, I know you all loved your dad equally, but the heart is a truly complicated thing."

I shift in my seat, simultaneously taking in her words and trying to push them away. She's giving me way too much credit.

And I have an Uber to catch.

"Baby, look at me."

My muscles obey without my permission. My own eyes stare back at me and I swallow thickly.

She squeezes my hand with surprising strength. "I promise you—and I'll swear on anything you want me to —*it's worth it.*"

My nose stings and the tears prick my eyes again.

"I wouldn't trade one single minute I spent with your dad to avoid the pain of losing him."

I swallow again. "I just..." But I don't know what comes after that.

"You can't run away from your own heart. It's like trying to escape your shadow. The only time it works is when you're living in darkness." Her voice is full of both conviction and warmth. I've missed her so damn much.

She holds my hand in both of hers as I breathe through the returning tightness in my chest until my lungs finally loosen their death grip.

Mama's brow furrows and she sends me a small smile. "And, besides, I need somebody on my side with this whole Ben Wheeler business. Your sister is determined to turn my hair gray."

I choke out a half-laugh/half-sob. "Yeah, I've been meaning to talk to somebody about that."

She sighs lightly, still with the smile. "So, what'll it be? Darkness or coming back into the fold?" Her thumb rubs over the back of my hand and I drop my eyes, watching the movement for a few beats.

"I've always been a fan of light," I finally say. Light and the wide-open spaces. I've never been a darkness kind of guy.

And I just happen to know exactly where I can find the sun.

The last time Rosie Carmichael tried to kiss me, she didn't even have a chance.

Because I was one step ahead of her and my lips were already on hers.

She claimed the concussion made her head light, but I know better.

~ THE END ~

Now that you've met Denny and Rosie, meet the rest of the family! ***Ale's Fair in Love and War*** (*Love on Tap*, Book 1) is now available. Stay tuned for an excerpt and grab your copy now!

We hope you enjoyed ***Full-On Clinger***, the prequel to the new ***Love on Tap*** series from Sylvie Stewart.

Want more stories from the *Love on Tap* crew? Check out

the ***Asheville Collection*** (Standalone Stories from the *Love on Tap* World)

Want another funny, swoon-worthy read from Sylvie Stewart? Try ***The Fix*** and start the addictive *Carolina Connections Series* now! FREE ebook for a limited time.

ALE'S FAIR IN LOVE AND WAR: An Enemies-to-Lovers Romance
Love on Tap, Book 1

Hollis Hayes is the worst neighbor in the entire history of neighbors.
She's also the hottest.
F.M.L.

I don't have time to fight with the dog groomer next door. There's a brewery to run, siblings to rein in, and a mom to look after. So if Hollis thinks I'll roll over and let her drive me out of business, she's not nearly as smart as she thinks she is.

Sure, I enjoy the little pranks we play on each other, and I don't hate watching her prance around in those tight leggings. But she's gone too far this time, even if she pretends to know nothing about it.

I'll do whatever it takes to save my business from going under, and if that means playing dirty with the girl I love to hate, game on.

If you like snarky banter, sizzling chemistry, big crazy families, and evil geniuses, **Ale's Fair in Love and War** *is* *your next weekend read. It is a standalone steamy romance with tons of heart and an HEA.*

ALE'S FAIR IN LOVE AND WAR

Chapter One: Virgin Says What?

CASH

"Blue Bigfoot Beer," I bark into the phone, tucking the receiver between my shoulder and ear. The customer across from me holds out his hand as I count his change from the drawer.

A breathy voice on the other end of the line has my hand freezing in midair.

"Is this Cash?" she purrs.

Hmm. Seems like my day might be about to turn around.

I drop the change into the customer's palm and toss him a chin lift.

"That's me. What can I do for you?" I have a few ideas if the voice matches the body.

She lets out a little giggle that has my dick twitching in my jeans. "I'm calling about your virginity."

My hearing must be going because it sounded like she just called me a virgin.

Turning away from the prying eyes of my brother a few

feet down the bar, I take the receiver in hand and press it firmly to my ear this time. "Sorry, come again?"

"Your virginity," she repeats, her voice still filled with sex but carrying a tinge of amusement now. "I'm interested in relieving you of it."

I squint at my reflection in the mirror of the back bar, wondering if I always look this tired and trying to figure out which of my three brothers is fucking with me. I settle on Denver because that asshole has been way too jolly ever since he got his girlfriend to move in with him.

"Very funny, Rosie. Tell Denny I'm gonna kick his ass next time I see him." The phone drops back in its cradle with a heavy *clang*. I don't have time for jokes today. There's a brewery to run, a taproom to serve, a newbie to train, and a pale ale release tomorrow that I'm not even close to being ready for.

I glance down the bar just in time to see my youngest brother, Miller, slosh water all over the floor mats as he drains the sink. The towel I throw at him hits him square in the face. "You *trying* to create a hazard or does it just come naturally?"

He sends a glare over his shoulder, a new eyebrow piercing glinting at me as I brush past him to serve another customer. This guy is a regular, so there's no need to ask for his order. I press a pint glass onto the cold rinse and pull back the tap on Squatch This, a smooth wheat with a sweet finish.

The phone rings again, and I'm somewhat encouraged to see Miller answer it unprompted while I finish with Dale, the regular.

"It's for you." My little brother thrusts the phone in my direction.

I gesture for him to make the rounds of the taproom as I grab the receiver. If I've got to work with him, I'm at least gonna train him right. Family can be a real pain in the ass sometimes.

"This is Cash."

"Oh, uh, hey." The masculine voice on the other end stumbles. I'd half expected it to be Denny cackling at his own stupid joke, but this voice doesn't belong to anyone I know. I wait for him to speak, but time is money.

"Who is this?" I demand, knowing I'm taking my busy day out on a stranger and hearing my mama's voice in my head urging me to be patient. It's never been my strong suit.

"Tom."

I rack my brain looking for any trace of a Tom but can't recall a soul apart from the guy who runs the smoke shop a couple spaces down. This is *not* that Tom. I know this because *that* Tom is always high as a fucking kite and only refers to me as "Cool Money."

"Do I know you?" I glance out into the taproom to see Miller parked on his ass at a four top of attractive brunettes. That little...

"Uh, no," Tom mutters.

Jesus, it's like pulling teeth with this guy. "What can I do for you, Tom?" I repeat, impatience bleeding through.

"I was, uh, hoping *I* could do something for *you*."

For the love of Larry.

My eyelids drop closed as I brace a hip against the back bar. "Oh yeah." This time it's annoyance leading the charge. "What exactly can you do for me, *Tom*?"

"Pop your cherry."

When the receiver hits the phone's base this time, the clattering echoes through the entire taproom.

Someone is definitely fucking with me.

And I'm pretty sure I know who.

Recognizing the look on my face and the mood it signifies, Miller hauls ass back behind the bar, hiking his jeans up his hips as he goes. My little brother's contempt for belts is one of life's greater mysteries.

I take my agitation out on the bar, scrubbing the polyurethane finish with my bar towel until it gleams. The ring of the phone has my molars gnashing, and I leave the receiver right where it is.

"Aren't you gonna get that?" Miller asks.

"Don't touch it!" I throw the towel onto my shoulder and stalk down the hall to the office.

If she wants to start something, I'll make damn sure she regrets it. My eyes narrow to slits as they attempt to bore a hole through the wall separating my brewery from the neighboring pet groomer.

Happy Tails Salon. The name is just as sickly sweet as her fake-ass smiles and fluttering eyelashes behind those misleadingly innocent glasses.

Miller's disembodied voice breaks through the speaker of the desk phone. "It's Mama, jackass. Line 2."

Well, shit.

"Hey, Mama." I do my best to brush off my irritation. Mama doesn't need to know about any of my troubles.

"Hello, baby. How are you?" Her concerned tone has me immediately wary. My eyes dart around the office, but I haven't one damn clue what I'm expecting to find.

"I'm great. How are you? Did you find Mango?" Mango is Mama's true baby, and everyone knows it.

She clucks her tongue. "You know, he just showed up in the kitchen a few minutes after you left. I don't know what he got himself into, but he's here now, safe and sound. *Aren't you, my little sweetheart?*" she coos at the critter, and I realize I'm just being paranoid.

"That's good to hear." I glance at my watch. "Hey, aren't you gonna be late for work?" It's already halfway through the afternoon and I haven't gotten shit done.

"I'm leaving in a few," she replies. "I just wanted to call about your... problem."

My butt drops into the desk chair, and I smile into the phone. "I wouldn't say he's *my* problem. I like to think of Miller as *all of our* problem."

"Oh hush, you. I'm not talking about your brother— although I am so glad you took my suggestion and hired him."

Took her suggestion? More like folded to her edict. Hiring Miller was not my idea at all, but the idiot crashed his bike and got fired from yet another job, so my hands were well and truly tied. Blue Bigfoot Beer is a family venture in many ways, but my oldest brother, Carter, and I are the only ones left holding the bag at the end of the day.

"Yeah, well." There wasn't much more to say than that.

Mama did always teach us if you don't have something nice to say, don't say anything at all. "So, what problem are you talking about?"

"Your virginity, sweetheart."

Fuck. My. Life.

Twenty minutes later, I'm staring at a Craigslist ad on my laptop that has both my name and Blue Bigfoot's phone number on it.

"Looking for someone gentle to break my guymen. I just haven't met the right person, and it's become a burden. Please be kind because I'm hideously ugly."

"Dude, there are easier ways."

Miller's voice sends me jumping. The bastard is leaning over my shoulder reading the screen and breathing his nicotine dragon breath in my face. I give him a good shove.

"Fuck off. I didn't post this," I grunt. "And who's manning the bar?"

Hitching his jeans up again, he snickers, enjoying this way more than I'd like. "Relax. Oscar's got it covered."

I only glare in response. There's no way I'm telling him that Mama just offered the services of her buddy Regina to help me out with my so-called problem. The same Regina who runs an escort service catering to Asheville's elite and hard up.

Of which I'm neither, thank you very much.

"Any idea who did it?" Miller flicks his tongue ring against his teeth, sending my already raw nerve endings buzzing.

There's only one person on this earth who can get

under my skin and make me take my eye off the ball like this.

I grit my teeth around my growl of an answer. "*Hollis.*"

Find out what happens next in ***Ale's Fair in Love and War: An Enemies-to-Lovers Romance***.

www.sylviestewartauthor.com

Excerpt from The Fix

My life is a friggin' fairytale—just not the kind any single girl would ever want to star in.

LANEY:

Like any good heroine, I have challenges to face. Getting my son to wear pants is one; dealing with my snooze-fest of a job is another. Then there's the Beast, my freeloading brother who's worn a permanent dent in the couch at my new place. And no fairytale would be complete without a smoking hot prince, of course. Too bad he's a complete ass.

My instincts scream at me to steer clear of Nate Murphy. Because, if life has taught me anything, there is no such thing as happily ever after.

NATE:

I may not be a superhero, but I do my best to come to the rescue when I'm needed. And, hey, I just moved halfway across the country after a single phone call from my mom. But being back home and taking on the responsibilities involved makes me a bit cranky at times. Unfortunately, the one time I completely lose my cool is in front of the hottest girl I've ever met. I've got my work cut out for me if I'm going to fix this. But I *will* fix this.

I'll be anything Laney Monroe needs me to be ... a superhero, a prince, or just a guy she might take a chance on.

Chapter Fourteen: *Scarlett O'Hara Had an Excellent Point*

LANEY

I ran my tongue around the shell of his ear and sucked his earlobe. Apparently that was the last straw. Nate physically picked me up and headed to my bedroom with his hands on my ass, and I had no choice but to hang on for dear life. This was shocking and a bit embarrassing on many levels, the least of which being the chronically untidy state of my bedroom.

Let me explain.

In all these romance novels, the buff guys are constantly picking the girls up and throwing them on the bed or having vertical make-out sessions—all while not straining a single muscle. I am not that girl. I have tits and I have ass, and I'm not saying that in some cute little "oh, look at her perky booty" kind of way. I have triple Ds and a very proportionate ass to match. That very often puts me into the plus-size department and then on to a tailor to fit the smaller parts of me. Everyone loves to talk about boobs and booty like they are thrilled the old bombshell figure is back in style, but I can tell you two things: (1) a rack like this wreaks havoc on your back, and (2) tailors are not inexpensive.

So Nate carrying me to my bedroom, an event which should have been a romantic milestone complete with "Up Where We Belong" playing in the background, was instead an episode that filled me with self-doubt and imagined trips to the emergency room. A hernia, at the very least, was a distinct possibility in this little scenario—how romantic can you get?

Amazingly, though, we made it without injury and he deposited me gently on the bed. He honestly didn't look any worse for wear, and his lustful look implied I'd better kick my insecurities to the curb. Shit was about to get real. *Yowza!*

Grab your copy of ***The Fix*** and start the award-winning *Carolina Connections* series today! Free ebook for a limited time: www.sylviestewartauthor.com

Also by Sylvie Stewart

Thanks and Keep in Touch

Thank you so much for reading **Full-On Clinger**. Continue the *Love on Tap* series with Cash and Hollis' story in ***Ale's Fair in Love and War: an enemies-to-lovers romance.***

Subscribe to my newsletter for updates, sales, giveaways, and free stuff! http://bit.ly/focnl

Come hang out with me!
Join my **Reader Group** on Facebook: www.facebook.com/groups/SylviesSpot

Stay up to date and keep in touch!

- www.sylviestewartauthor.com
- sylvie@sylviestewartauthor.com
- Facebook: SylvieStewartAuthor
- Twitter: @sylvie_stewart_

- Instagram: sylvie.stewart.romance
- BookBub: sylvie-stewart
- Goodreads: bit.ly/ss_gr
- Pinterest: @sylviestewartauthor
- TikTok: @authorsylviestewart

XOXO,
Sylvie

About the Author

USA Today bestselling author Sylvie Stewart loves dad jokes, hot HEAs, country music, and baby skunks—preferably all at the same time. Most of her steamy romantic comedies take place in North Carolina, a.k.a. the best state ever, and she's a sucker for hugs from her kids and a good laugh with her hubby. She also cusses like a sailor and can't bring herself to feel bad about it. If you love smart Southern gals, hot blue-collar guys, and snort-laughing with characters who feel like your best friends, Sylvie's your gal.

facebook.com/SylvieStewartAuthor

twitter.com/sylvie_stewart_

instagram.com/sylvie.stewart.romance

bookbub.com/authors/sylvie-stewart

tiktok.com/@authorsylviestewart

52647912R00071